Joanna Thompson

Long Distance Kisses

Planet Girl

50/50

Did you ever have writer's **block**? No, me neither – until now. It's a terrible thing. I've been back at school in London for less than a week and already I'm sitting in front of a computer screen wishing I were somewhere else. Anywhere but Chalk Farm School for Girls in London. Hull, maybe. Mogadishu, perhaps. I have one of those stupid *What I did in the summer* essays to do for my English teacher, Mr Benn, and I feel sick every time I look at my **blank** screen. My fingers won't type.

+++ block – Blockade +++ blank – leer +++

One reason my fingers and my brain are on strike is that I've just had a *really* complicated summer. Being a famous international playgirl, I spent my holidays in two different places: Berlin and Scotland. If that doesn't *sound* too complicated, **trust** me – it was. My summer holiday experiences have left me confused. It feels like I left half of myself in Scotland and the other half in Berlin, which leaves … none of me in London, *oder*? That would explain why I can't write my essay! What did *I do*, Mr Benn? I hardly even know who *I am* at the moment, Mr Benn.

For anyone else out there who doesn't know who *I* am, *I* am **supposed to** be Emily Hausmann. I'm 50% English and 50% German, which is sometimes really great and sometimes really a problem. Right now, it seems really tricky. Anyway, 100% of me left Berlin last year to come here to Chalk Farm School for Girls, a **posh** boarding school in London.

I shouldn't really still be here at all, **struggling** with my essay and confusion right now. The school year in London that my rich grandmother had paid for was officially over two months ago, in July. I'd done it all: Survived living in a **dorm** with a bizarre group of girls? *Tick.* Had my heart broken? *Tick.* Been the subject of at least one blog? *Tick.* Fallen in love again? *Tick.* Made great friends? *Tick.* Made a couple of real enemies? *Tick.* Got good grades? Well, anyway, you get the idea.

+++ to trust – vertrauen +++ to be supposed to – sollen +++
posh – reich +++ to struggle – kämpfen +++ dorm – Schlafsaal +++
Tick. – Abgehakt. +++

It was time, in other words, to go back to Berlin, to my friends there, my school, my family, with my head held high and **loads of** cool stories to tell. But I didn't. I decided to stay on in London instead.

I can remember the *exact* moment that I decided to stay in London, in fact. I was in a cupboard. Yes, that's right. A cupboard. I was in a cupboard kissing a boy named Sam, to be very precise. Even more precisely – a cute boy named Sam whom I had been dating for a few months. We ended up in the cupboard just after he played drums with his band, the Kitty Gagarins, for the last time. He was now getting ready to leave London and go back to his hometown in Scotland **for good**.

Yes, you heard me right and, no, it doesn't make any sense. I decided to stay on at Chalk Farm School for another year **even though** the boy I loved was leaving. Effectively, I decided to stay in London to be "with" a boy who would **actually** be living 667 km away.

Sam wasn't **heading** home to make my love life complicated, of course. The real reason was that his dad had lost his job and his family couldn't pay Sam's enormous **fees** at St Dougan's, the boys' school across the street, any more. That didn't stop Sam and me wanting to be together, though. Me being in London **rather** than Berlin seemed to *sort of* make sense: at least we would be on the same island!

+++ loads of – jede Menge +++ for good – endgültig +++ even though – obwohl +++ actually – eigentlich +++ to head – *hier:* gehen +++ fee – Gebühr +++ rather – eher +++

So we agreed to keep our relationship going – long distance love. It sounded quite romantic – *on paper*. We had it all planned out – *on paper*. But events over the summer have made everything more difficult, like I said. I'm so **guilty** about everything that I hate myself, I really do. And I keep wondering about the "cupboard **decision**": was it the right one? Did it really make sense? Did I stay in London for the right reasons?

I give up with my essay for Mr Benn. I can't tell him what happened. I can, sort of, tell you – if you'll give me time. For any of this story to make sense, you'll have to remember that I am confused. I need to talk to someone first about the summer, sit down and go through everything until it comes together.

For the other 50%, the German part, you'll just have to wait a bit. Oh come on, it won't kill you.

+++ guilty – schuldig +++ decision – Entscheidung +++

50% of what I did this Summer

Hmmm, Maths is not absolutely my best subject, of course. I spent ten days out of a total of six weeks of summer holidays in Scotland. That's not 50%, right? Still, it felt like it. It was a beautiful time, really.

The trip up north was Sam's **treat**. He'd joked about showing me round his homeland even as we kissed in the cupboard. He'd then surprised me with a **coach** ticket to Glasgow two weeks later, luckily just before I bought my flight back to Berlin for the summer.

But, **steady**, Hausmann. Let's start at the beginning. If I close my eyes, I'm back in the summer …

First and worst: I have to tell my parents about my trip to Sam's, of course, which is *really* **embarrassing**: *Yes, Mum, I am coming home but, well, would it be OK if I were ten days late and went to Scotland with a boy named Sam? Yes, we are … going out. Yes, I can trust him. Yes, his parents will be there.* You get the idea. Mum and Dad are confused – *Emily actually has a boyfriend?* – and **suspicious** but finally they agree to let me book me a flight from

---

✦✦✦ treat – besonderes Vergnügen ✦✦✦ coach – Bus ✦✦✦ steady – langsam ✦✦✦ embarrassing – peinlich ✦✦✦ suspicious – misstrauisch ✦✦✦

Glasgow to Berlin and arrive back in the Motherland later than planned. Phew!

After that **nightmare** is over, I am free to count off the final, totally boring days of **term** until we can leave. I can hardly wait! Scotland! It must be so romantic, right? **Misty** valleys and green hills, deep **lochs** with monsters and ... emm, Mel Gibson and stuff. Like I said, *romantic*.

My dream trip gets off to a less than *romantic* start, unfortunately. Sam and me were supposed to meet outside St Dougan's so I could help him carry some of his luggage. Leaving London for good will mean that Sam has to take everything he owns with him. *By coach*. The coach driver is a friend of Sam's "Uncle Johnny", apparently, and will **turn a blind eye to** "a bit of extra stuff", Sam told me. Hmmm. Something tells me it will be more than "a bit".

In the end, though, I make my own way to Victoria Coach Station, after Sam texts me to say he's **running late**. In code: his text reads: *Rnnig L8 go station wout me. big pT last nite v tired. xxx* I translate it to mean that the boys in Sam's house held a massive **farewell** party for him last night which went on till late, or rather early – early *this morning*. From his text message, I'd say Sam didn't go to bed at all, actually.

Ten minutes before the coach is about to leave and just as I'm actually starting to wonder if I'll be taking the high

---

+++ nightmare – Albtraum +++ term – Schulhalbjahr
+++ misty – neblig +++ loch – See +++ to turn a blind eye to –
bei etw. ein Auge zudrücken +++ to run late – spät dran sein +++
farewell – Abschied +++

road to Scotland by myself, Sam finally arrives. He's a funny **sight**.

Just as I'd feared, Sam's got his whole life in London, all three years of it, hanging from his body, like he's a pack **mule**. His life seems to be made up of a black rucksack, a pot plant, some **cymbals**, and two plastic bags, hung over his arms. Sam **staggers** towards me, like someone who's been **stabbed** in the back and is trying to get to help. He almost falls into my arms.

I'm just wondering if I should call an ambulance/Scotland Yard when I notice that Sam's band mates from the Kitty Gagarins are following him. They all look very tired and very green and seem to be carrying *even more of Sam's stuff*. Nightmare.

At the head of the caravan of Kermit-skinned boys is Ed Stanton, the guitarist in the band and my ex-boyfriend. Ed's holding what looks like a CD **rack** and he seems confused. He stares at the rack, as if he's trying to remember why he's carrying it, and then looks round himself in horror: I think he can't quite believe that people *actually travel together in large coaches*. Ed's obviously never been in a coach station in his life before. Coach travel is for poor people, after all, and Ed's a real rich kid.

I **gulp**. Ed and me have *sort of* left the past behind us now. We have spoken a couple of times since he finished with me and then **boasted** about it in his "Babe Blog" all

---

+++ sight – *hier:* Anblick +++ mule – Maultier +++ cymbal – Becken (Schlagzeug) +++ to stagger – taumeln +++ to stab – erstechen +++ rack – Ständer +++ to gulp – schlucken +++ to boast – angeben +++

those months ago. He still makes me **uneasy**, though. Sam swears Ed's a "new man" with a **steady** girlfriend whom he treats well. But call it feminine intuition – I don't trust him. And I think he doesn't totally trust me either. He's put the CD rack down next to me and is giving me probably exactly the same funny look that I'm giving him.

Steve, the singer from the band, is there, too, carrying one little rucksack and walking very slowly and carefully, rather as though he were wearing **high heels**. And Matt the bass player, Sam's best friend in London, and now officially my friend Maudie's new flame, is also there. He's now swinging yet another enormous bag onto the coach. "Thank God you used the school's drum kit," he puffs. "I wouldn't have **fancied** getting *that* over here."

Matt stands, hands on **hips**, trying to catch his breath. He looks really ill, too. Lord knows what they were all doing last night. Though even with skin the colour of **pond slime**, Matt's still a cute guy. He's a bit shorter than I thought he was, I realise, quite a bit shorter than the rest of the band. Shorter even than that stupid CD rack – *where's that going to go?* I **suspect** he's even smaller than Maudie, though she hasn't **mentioned** that. Which is odd, as she has talked about Matt all the flaming time since they started going out together.

The four boys are all just standing there, **gasping** and

+++ uneasy – unbehaglich +++ steady – *hier:* fest +++ high heels – hohe Absätze +++ to fancy – gern mögen +++ hip – Hüfte +++ pond slime – grünlicher Schlick +++ to suspect – vermuten +++ to mention – erwähnen +++ to gasp – nach Luft schnappen +++

groaning, when Sam finally manages to put a sentence together: "Maybe you should get on the coach and keep our seats?" he **croaks** to me. "I just want to say goodbye to the guys." I nod; the coach seems to be filling up. It would be **torture** to have to sit on a different seat from Sam. I'm hoping, *natürlich,* for a bit of kissing and **cuddling** action en route. If Sam lives long enough.

I wave at the three remaining members of the Kitty Gagarins and climb into the coach. By some miracle, I manage to find two empty places near the back and sink into the one nearest the window, putting my camera bag on the other seat to keep it for Sam. Yes, my camera bag. I love taking photos and I never leave home without my trusty old Pentax. Unlike Sam, I'm travelling light. I've left most of my stuff at school but my camera is, of course, *essential.*

I'm **tempted** to take a picture of the scene I can see out of the window now: the four band mates are standing together, their arms round each other, like American football stars before a big game. Ed is talking and Matt actually has his eyes closed – he looks a bit like he's *praying.* Then Sam says something and passes the pot plant he brought with him this morning to Matt! *Why?* Everyone laughs and they all **hug** again.

It's actually quite an emotional scene, for a group of cool boys. I can feel the beginnings of a **lump** in my

---

✦✦✦ to groan – stöhnen ✦✦✦ to croak – krächzen ✦✦✦ torture – Folter ✦✦✦ to cuddle – kuscheln ✦✦✦ essential – unentbehrlich ✦✦✦ to be tempted – in Versuchung sein ✦✦✦ to pray – beten ✦✦✦ to hug – (sich) umarmen ✦✦✦ lump – Klumpen ✦✦✦

throat. I think about what the band has meant to me, how **odd** it is to imagine them playing without Sam …

I close my eyes for a second and when I open them, Sam is finally joining me on board the coach – he's the last passenger to get on. He winks at the driver: "Alright, Sid?" and the coach finally moves off. I'm surprised it's possible with so much of Sam's stuff in the boot. How he got that CD rack in I'll never know.

We drive slowly out of the coach station, passing what's left of the Kitty Gagarins as they cross a small road. Sam waves quickly at them, then settles **properly** into his seat, putting his arm around me. Hmm, nice.

"Are you alright?" I ask quietly. It's difficult to read Sam sometimes. He's told me a million times that he's fine about going back to Scotland but I know he was happy in London, too. Sam nods. "I'd probably be really depressed if you weren't here." And then he adds, "All I really want to think about is not being sick right now! I'm so tired." Ah, boys! They're so sentimental.

Then, unfortunately, what could have been a "superb chance" to do lots of kissing becomes a "superb chance" to get to know the motorways of Northern England as Sam takes his glasses off, yawns and falls asleep immediately on my shoulder.

The journey to Scotland is a bit scary, for lots of reasons. It's scary firstly because it lasts **literally** *forever*. Don't

+++ odd – komisch +++ properly – richtig +++ literally – buchstäblich +++

laugh. Yes, I did know that England and Scotland were different countries, thanks. I just didn't *quite* realise that there are planets in the solar system that are closer to each other than London and Glasgow are. It takes *eight hours* until we're on the **outskirts** of Glasgow. I am *sooo* definitely flying next time, even if it's not very green. (We couldn't have gone by plane this time because Sam would have spent nine million pounds on **excess luggage**, of course.)

The other frightening thing about the journey is my own imagination. With Sam asleep, all I can really do for eight hours is stare at service stations/trees/more trees – and worry about meeting Sam's family. Sam is my first serious boyfriend so I've never had to do the "meet the parents" thing before. What if his mum and dad don't like me? What if they sense that I'm not the right girl for Sam?

I don't really know what to expect either. Sam loves his family, that's clear, but, well, between you and me, they seem to have rather a lot of problems. His parents are divorced, his dad is unemployed and has diabetes and the family don't seem to have much money. Oh, and Sam told me that the town just outside Glasgow where he's from was once voted the second worst place to live in Britain. It doesn't totally sound like I've got a fun holiday **ahead of** me, now does it?

So by the time Sam finally wakes up – unbelievably, at the precise moment that we pass a sign saying "Welcome

+++ outskirts – Stadtrand +++ excess luggage – Übergepäck +++ ahead of – vor +++

to Glasgow" – I've officially driven myself mad. Sam's dad is **due to** pick us up at the coach station and I'm now expecting a cross between Räuber Hotzenplotz and Dumbo (people who get diabetes are fat, right?) to be waiting for us, with a *Bollerwagen* attached to the back of his wheelchair to carry our luggage.

I'm certainly *not* expecting Sam to nod in the direction of a young, **handsome** and suspiciously healthy looking guy in his early forties when we finally get off the coach. It shouldn't really be a surprise – Sam's hot and he gets it from his dad, **plainly** – but still, like I say: it's a **relief**.

Sam's dad is not only "quite hot for a dad", he's also very friendly. He hugs first Sam, then me very hard and **insists** that I call him "Alan", which feels a bit strange the first couple of times I try to say it. I'm 50% German, remember. I still say "Sie" to my parents' best friends back in Berlin, even though I've known them since before I was born and they've seen me naked and things.

I try hard to get used to calling Mr Reid "Alan". "Alan" leads us to "Alan's" car – not a *Bollerwage*n, obviously, but a normal looking Ford. "Alan" has to fight to **squeeze** in all of Sam's luggage – especially that blooming CD rack, which is driving me *mad* – and then we're off to the second worst town in Britain, with "Alan" talking all the time. "Alan" is really nice and funny, it turns out.

You'll be pleased to hear that I'm now used to calling him "Alan".

✦✦✦ to be due to – sollen ✦✦✦ handsome – gut aussehend ✦✦✦ plainly – deutlich ✦✦✦ relief – Erleichterung ✦✦✦ to insist on – bestehen auf ✦✦✦ to squeeze – quetschen ✦✦✦

Cumbernauld, Sam's hometown, doesn't actually seem *that* bad. OK, it does remind me just a little bit of Eisenhüttenstadt, *die erste sozialistische Stadt*. Crazy Onkel Dieter, my dad's brother, lives there so I can tell you from first hand experience: Cumbernauld looks slightly like the DDR, circa 1982. A *lot* of *Plattenbau*. A *lot* of **concrete**.

We drive through even more concrete until we reach Sam's mum's house, a small, attractive **terraced** one, with a **neat** front garden. Sam's two younger brothers also live here with her: Sam will join them now, too. "Alan" has a small flat two streets away, it seems.

Sam's mum is waiting for us at the door of her house, welcoming us with a big smile and Sam's nose, I notice immediately. Her name is "Eileen" – as in "Just call me Eileen", of course. She's also friendly, kissing not just Sam and me but – get this – Sam's dad, too. They're, like, divorced. I didn't expect "Eileen" to **headbutt** "Alan" in the face or anything but still. **Weird**. Why split up if you still like each other so much?

It's very quickly clear: Sam's home life is *nothing* like the depressing Scottish episode of *Raus aus den Schulden* I'd imagined on the coach. I don't know what I had been thinking. Actually, I do: I had been thinking that I might be able to help poor Family Reid as they sat, crying into their *Schleimbrei*, in their Soviet-style concrete *Plattenbau*. That coach journey!

The problem is not just eight hours of coach worry.

+++ concrete – Beton +++ terraced house – Reihenhaus +++ neat – gepflegt +++ to headbutt – *hier*: sich gegenseitig die Köpfe einschlagen +++ weird – komisch +++

The problem is also going to a posh boarding school and being surrounded by girls who have **gold-plated** lives, I realise. I'm totally used to my roommates talking **casually** about things like their "stables" (Melissa) or their mother's "**cosmetic surgeons**" (Becks. I don't even want to *know* what kind of work Becks' mum's had done). I even – *sort of* – got used to Olga Petrova, our ex-roommate, talking about "Daddy's yacht" in the same kind of bored tone you'd say "Daddy's Opel Corsa". I've been living in a big **pound-shaped bubble** for the past year.

It's high time to **burst** it because it's clearly damaged my brain. When Sam told me about his parents not being able to pay for school in London any more, I "forgot" that the fees at St Dougan's are enormous – imagine buying an Opel Corsa every week and you're close – and it's not normal to have that kind of money. I *sooooo* need a reality check and I know that Scotland and Berlin are the right places to help me with this. I'm coming home. Twice.

At dinner I meet Sam's two brothers, Liam and Cameron. I'm relieved to see that they are normal young boys: they're **lunatics**. During the course of the meal, they're hungry, they're not hungry, they're happy, they're sad, they're loud, they're really quiet. They're just like my little brother, Max, in other words.

✦✦✦ gold-plated – vergoldet ✦✦✦ casually – beiläufig ✦✦✦ cosmetic surgeon – Schönheitschirurg ✦✦✦ pound-shaped bubble – Blase in der Form einer Pfundnote ✦✦✦ to burst – platzen lassen ✦✦✦ lunatic – Verrückte/r ✦✦✦

Eileen's cooked haggis for us to eat – Sam's "**hilarious**" idea, of course. He's been threatening me with haggis since we met, more or less. Haggis is Scotland's national dish. Hold on to your lunch – it's sheep's **stomach** mixed with *Haferflocken*. Sounds fingerlickin' good, eh?

As I lift the first forkful of haggis into my mouth, my hand shakes: it feels like Sam's whole family are watching me carefully. Eileen probably has a bucket ready, just in case I **vomit**. I don't need it, luckily: haggis is surprisingly tasty. But as Sam looks over and grins at me, I do swear to myself that if he ever comes to Germany, I'll get my dad to bake a lovely *Eisbein und Blutwurst* pie or something.

After I've passed my Scottish "**initiation** test", the meal is relaxed. "Alan" does most of the talking, **cracking a joke** every second minute. He doesn't seem depressed. He doesn't seem ill either, though I notice he doesn't eat dessert. And he tells a story about Sam getting lost in the local supermarket as a small boy, which is very, very funny **indeed**, **unless** your name is "Sam".

When we've all finished eating, Sam's brothers disappear to play their X-box upstairs. It's my turn to talk now. Sam's parents are curious about Berlin – people are always curious about Berlin – and especially curious about the fact that my dad's family come from East Germany. They want to know how life there was. I can't say, *well, it looked a bit like here, actually,* and Sam's parents

---

✦✦✦ hilarious – lustig ✦✦✦ stomach – Magen ✦✦✦ to vomit – sich übergeben ✦✦✦ initiation – Einführung ✦✦✦ to crack a joke – einen Witz reißen ✦✦✦ indeed – zwar ✦✦✦ unless – außer, wenn ✦✦✦

don't seem to *quite* understand that the DDR was long gone before I was born, so I just **make** some things **up**. I'm good at that.

It's late when Alan finally disappears, kissing Eileen so often that I'm scared she'll start bleeding. It's not fair – why should divorced people get to do all the kissing? I haven't kissed Sam all day and even if we do have a chance later, I'm getting dangerously tired.

Sam on the other hand, having slept for eight hours on the coach, is **disgustingly** lively. He's even singing as he helps Eileen to set up a comfortable looking cream-coloured sofa bed for me to sleep on in the living room. Then Eileen heads upstairs, **winking** as she goes. "Don't stay up talking all night! Or doing anything else!"

When she's safely out of sight, Sam and me quickly jump onto the sofa bed. I'm hoping, **frankly**, that Sam will start kissing me **straight away** so that I can then go to sleep as soon as possible but – nightmare – he seems to want to *talk* instead.

It's **cruel**. Sam's not normally what you'd call a big conversationalist but tonight, it seems, he's analysing *every* aspect of *everything*. It's been a big day for him, of course, and I do understand why he needs to talk about some things: how he felt as he left London – sad but relieved – **for instance**. I'm not really sure why we have to talk now, at 11.56 pm, about how I feel about going back for another year at Chalk Farm School – good and bad. (I'm

+++ to make sth up – etw. erfinden +++ disgusting – ekelhaft +++ to wink – zwinkern +++ frankly – offen gesagt +++ straight away – sofort +++ cruel – grausam +++ for instance – zum Beispiel +++

Miss 50/50, don't forget.) I'm not sure why we have to go through how I feel about sharing a dorm with Amanda Dobson, the prize **bitch** at my school. We call her **Cyclops** because she has one eye slightly bigger than the other, ever since she had an "accident" playing hockey years ago. And because she really is a monster.

"I'll survive," I yawn. I think Sam feels responsible for me. He knows he's the main reason I'm staying on in London and if I have a bad time there, it will be his fault. It won't be, of course … it was my … oh, can feel my eyes *cloooosiiinnnggg*. Sam suddenly says, "OK, I can see you're **whacked**! I've just got to ask one more thing: what do you think of my family?"

I think guiltily about my bizarre Dumbo/Räuber Hotzenplotz fantasy. No need to mention that, I don't believe. I **mumble** something instead about Eileen and Alan seeming *great, really down to earth* …

Sam knows what I mean. He nods. "Yeah, it's nice to be back in the real world." He rolls his eyes. "Most kids at private schools have no idea what life is actually like. I suppose there were a few people in London whose parents didn't live in palaces or castles."

"Me," I say, simply. I think about my family's flat in Berlin. It's nice and I miss it, actually, but it's nothing special. And – the horror – it's *rented*. Melissa nearly **fainted** when I told her that. In Britain, if you don't own your house, you're not even Hartz IV – you're Hartz MMCV.

✦✦✦ bitch – Miststück ✦✦✦ Cyclops – Zyklop ✦✦✦ to be whacked – am Ende sein ✦✦✦ to mumble – murmeln ✦✦✦ to faint – ohnmächtig werden ✦✦✦

Sam smiles at me. "Yeah, you, of course. You're fine, even if your Grandma is pretty much England's richest woman, by the sound of it." The Queen Mother actually offered to help Sam with his school fees last term. He didn't take the money. "She could probably buy half of Scotland if she wanted …"

"She wouldn't want to," I interrupt, with a serious face. "Too many **peasants**."

Sam grins and says in a serious voice, "Fancy kissing a peasant, Madam?"

"Madam" does and "Madam" then finally spends a good 20 minutes getting very close to one of the *Lumpenproletariat*. And when her favourite Scottish peasant finally disappears upstairs, "Madam" **barely** sees him go. "Madam's" **unconscious**.

The next few days in Scotland gallop past. Sam and me do loads of great stuff. We go on a lot of day trips to other places: Glasgow, Edinburgh and St Andrews, a beautiful small town on the east coast, with a **gorgeous** beach. We buy a **kite** there. Yes, a kite, one of those things that people under ten love so much. There's not enough wind to fly it and Sam ends up **dragging** it along the sand, while I laugh so hard that I almost need an operation to **stitch** me back together afterwards.

It's a cruel, cruel world, though, and far too soon it's my last night in Scotland. The evening before I'm due to

---

+++ peasant – Bauer +++ barely – kaum +++ unconscious – besinnungslos +++ gorgeous – wunderschön +++ kite – Drachen +++ to drag – ziehen +++ to stitch – nähen +++

fly back to Berlin, Sam and me sit up till late on my sofa bed, planning "Operation Long Distance Love". Sam has worked out an **impressive schedule** for us, with us each taking it in turns to visit the other once a month.

"Operation Long Distance Love" sounds great, really exciting. If Sam and me are crazy about each other now, just think how we'll feel after a couple of weeks apart! **Absence** makes the heart grow **fonder**. *Die Liebe wächst mit der Entfernung.* All of that. It's perfect, **apart from** the fact that the coach trip is hellish, of course. That's the only thing we argue about. Sam tells me a bit **sniffily** it's *not environmentally friendly to fly and* it's *too expensive*. All I

✦✦✦ impressive – beeindruckend ✦✦✦ schedule – Plan ✦✦✦ absence – Abwesenheit ✦✦✦ fond – *hier:* verliebt ✦✦✦ apart from – abgesehen von ✦✦✦ sniffy – hochnäsig, verächtlich ✦✦✦

can think is that I will manage the **occasional** flight even if it kills me.

Sam's about to go up to bed when it happens. The moment that **haunts** me most now. He looks at me long and hard and whispers gently, "We can make this work. You can trust me."

I stare straight back at Sam, right into his lovely blue eyes, and say, "You can trust me, too." Of course he can, right? I've got moral **integrity**. I'm your go-to girl for trust.

When I tell Sam that he can trust me, it's not a lie. I believe it then. And I believe it all the time I'm travelling back to Berlin, getting on a plane in Glasgow, meeting my parents at the airport, driving home, meeting up with Betti and Merle again, hanging out with them – I still believe it. I'm Sam's. We're bound together.

I only really stop believing that I'm someone you can trust in Mauerpark, Berlin, on 27th July this year. But now we're already getting to the part of "What I did in the summer holidays" that, actually, I really don't want to talk about now. So I'm not going to. Let's just jump forward a bit and go back to London. Thanks.

✦✦✦ occasional – gelegentlich ✦✦✦ to haunt – verfolgen ✦✦✦ integrity – Rechtschaffenheit ✦✦✦

Dumped by Text, Part Two

I arrive back in London to start on *Chalk Farm School: The Sequel* after four weeks in Berlin, feeling terribly, terribly guilty. (Look, I know I'm being mysterious but sometimes a girl just needs time to **get her head around things**, OK?) Anyway, luckily, there is a **distraction** almost immediately after I arrive.

As soon as I'm in the airport terminal, I switch my mobile on. I'm a bit nervous, as usual, as I do so: phones can cause you such pain sometimes. I remember when Ed Stanton dumped me by text, for instance, I felt like throwing my poor phone against the wall. And now, here we go again: I get a text message to tell me that I've been dumped again. Only this time, I could kiss my lovely phone. I'm ecstatic.

The text is from Maudie and the news is amazing: *Cyclops is talking about her brilliant new dorm on Facebook! Says dorm 3B **a bunch of** losers! Looks like she's **out of your hair**. See you soon, loser!*

+++ to dump s. b. – *hier:* Schluss machen +++ sequel – Fortsetzung +++ to get one's head around things – sich über etw. klar werden +++ distraction – Ablenkung +++ a bunch of – ein Haufen +++ to be out of s. b.'s hair – jmdm. nicht mehr auf der Pelle hocken +++

God bless Maudie, my window on the world. Ever since Amanda "Cyclops" Dobson stole the boy Maudie was interested in last term, Rob, she has been following Cyclops' every move online. "I know when Cyclops **gets a hot wax**, I know when she goes to the toilet," Maudie once growled at me. She was only half joking. Luckily, it's easy to know about Cyclops' every move **as**, ever since she got herself a BlackBerry last term, she's been all over cyberspace, networking her **evil** heart out. I think Maudie's still **scared stiff** that Cyclops will go after Matt, even though Matt's far too cool and smart to fall for Cyclops.

I trust Maudie's information but I still won't believe Amanda's out of the dorm until I see it for myself. I'm sure Cyclops knows that Maudie's got a cyber-eye on her. Maybe this is just a sick joke. But when I open the door to dorm 3B, I know it's really true. I notice it **instantly** – the place just smells different. It doesn't smell of anything.

Before Amanda Dobson moved in, dorm 3B did have its own aroma, of course: a harmless, pleasant one, of four different deos, perfumes and egos. Sometimes the place could get a *bit* sweaty, from Becks, 3B's "Sporty Spice", having spent too long in the gym. It occasionally smelt a *bit* horsey, when Melissa had returned from a weekend cleaning out stables at home. Nothing **offensive**, though. But all that changed when Amanda arrived with her mountains of potpourri and the world's largest

---

✦✦✦ to get a hot wax – sich die Haare mit Wachs entfernen ✦✦✦ as – da, weil ✦✦✦ evil – bösartig ✦✦✦ to be scared stiff – eine Heidenangst haben ✦✦✦ instantly – sofort ✦✦✦ offensive – widerwärtig ✦✦✦

orange-scented candle. Our dorm started to smell like a **massage parlour** and, trust me, not the good kind.

But now, *eau de bordell* has suddenly **vanished**. The big stupid candle has gone. The giant baby picture which hung above Cyclops' bed has gone. Amanda's huge **dresser**, which took up all the space and oxygen in the room, has gone. The sheepskin **rug** that I *hated* so much has also gone.

Everything that was Amanda's has disappeared. That can only mean one thing … oh, this is too good, there must be a **catch**! Amanda can't just have given up. She took so much pleasure in making me unhappy! And, of course, if it really is true, the next interesting question is: who's now sleeping in her bed?

I look carefully at the bed. It looks so ordinary but it's actually **cursed**, of course. Before Amanda, it was home to Olga Petrova, sort-of-evil-sort-of-Russian-American-genius who left London for Florida to get married – yes, really. She did. Now it's home to another … what? A mad dictator? A **swamp** monster?

I look around desperately for clues – swamp grass, slime – and then I **spot** it. "It" makes me breathe again, no, **strike** that! "It" makes me *smile* again. "It" is a book called: *How to Learn to Love Yourself*. I know whose book that is. I've seen someone carrying it around a lot. Some-

---

✦✦✦ orange-scented – nach Orange riechend ✦✦✦ massage parlour – Massagesalon ✦✦✦ to vanish – verschwinden ✦✦✦ dresser – Frisierkommode ✦✦✦ rug – Teppich ✦✦✦ catch – *hier:* Haken ✦✦✦ to curse – verfluchen ✦✦✦ swamp – Moor ✦✦✦ to spot – sehen ✦✦✦ to strike – *hier:* streichen, löschen ✦✦✦

one who really, of course, doesn't love herself but who, right now, I feel like I love more than anyone else in the world.

It's Sadie's book. Sadie is a girl in our class. She's just a normal girl. She's not a bitch, or a millionaire's daughter. She's possibly not the sharpest knife in the drawer, as they like to say here, but she's kind. **Decent**. Ethical.

Sadie, I think, in wonder. "*Sadie*," I say out loud and a posh voice behind me **yelps**, "Yes, darling, isn't it wonderful?" I jump and turn **in fright**, in an impressive Riverdance-style move, and there's Melissa. She must have been in our bathroom, which will actually have some space in it again now Amanda and her Amazing Technicoloured Collection of Beauty Products have gone! Wahaay!

Melissa comes over and hugs me and then **giggles**. Then she giggles again. "I had no idea Cyclops had gone until I got back yesterday! It was all arranged during the last week of the holidays, apparently. Sadie says she got a call from Miss Shaw asking if she would **swap** dormitories with Amanda. Cyclops asked to be moved from here. *Cyclops asked*, can you believe it?"

Melissa is now hugging herself, lost in **rapture**. "She's gone to dorm 8D now. Second floor," she adds helpfully, seeing my confused expression. I never know who's in which dorm. Melissa then says, a bit impatiently, "Cyclops is sharing with Laurie now." Laurie is Amanda Dobson's best friend/slave. How nice for them.

+++ decent – bescheiden +++ to yelp – aufschreien +++ in fright – erschrocken +++ to giggle – kichern +++ to swap – tauschen +++ rapture – Begeisterung +++

I wouldn't care if Cyclops were sleeping under a bridge, frankly. I just care that she's not sleeping here. I just care that I'll be sharing with Sadie. Lovely sweet, harmless Sadie. "How is Sadie?" I say, **fondly**, as though I were her auntie or something.

Melissa smiles and says, *Oh fine,* but looks a bit **vague**. I suspect that Melissa's not *that* interested in Sadie. She's just so happy to have "Switzerland" instead of "Iran" in the dorm. Sadie won't cause trouble. There will be no special emergency meetings of the UN Security Council, Chalk Farm Division, because of Sadie. I hope.

And there's one more thing. Melissa is whispering now, "Miss Shaw had to sort out all the dormitory swap-

+++ fond – liebevoll +++ vague – unbestimmt, wage +++

ping because *Miss Bardwell is still away* on her spiritual **retreat** in Japan and *she isn't coming back for at least six more weeks!*"

Miss Bardwell is our housemistress and Latin teacher, of course, who disappeared to Asia last term to "find herself" after having her heart broken by Mr Michaels, her ex-**fiancé** and one of the teachers at St Dougan's. My Auntie Nora was somehow involved in this heartbreaking and as a result Miss Bardwell hates anyone who has even **a speck of** Nora's DNA. Like – me, her niece. So her still being away is also truly great news.

Melissa winks. "So shall we go and celebrate? The cakes are on me!"

✦✦✦ retreat – Rückzug ✦✦✦ fiancé/e – Verlobte/r ✦✦✦ a speck of – ein Minimum, ein Körnchen ✦✦✦

Hier ist die Welt doch (nicht) in Ordnung

It's actually really nice to be asked out by Melissa like this. We get on well but last year there seemed to be so much happening, what with the Olga Petrova scandal and my, ahem, *complex* love life that I felt like I hardly saw her.

But now we're **making up for** lost time. Melissa and me **skip** down Chalk Farm Road, in the manner of people just out of prison. Unfortunately, we skip right past White Out, the café that was the centre of my London universe last year. Nearly every important event in my life took place here: my first date with Ed Stanton and loads of dates with Sam, for instance. My Auntie Nora and Mr Michaels, Miss Bardwell's ex-fiancé, met at White Out after their legendary kiss at the Kensington Christmas party. (The kiss that was heard around the whole school – it meant the end of Miss Bardwell's **engagement**.) Ah, sweet memories ... I'd love to go in. White Out is owned by a former boxer, Mr White, and I can see him now, playfully **punching** a customer in the head.

But Melissa is a lady and being punched in the head is

✦✦✦ to make up for s. th. – etw. aufholen ✦✦✦ to skip – hüpfen ✦✦✦ engagement – Verlobung ✦✦✦ to punch – boxen ✦✦✦

not **her cup of tea**; also a shame, as White Out do *wicked* cups of tea, so strong they take the **enamel** off your teeth. Just the way I like it.

It seems Melissa is taking me instead to her favourite posh ladies' café. It's called Toast and it's famous at school for being the place where the "horsey set" hang out. As, personally, I am about as "horsey" as a fish, I've never set foot in Toast – until now …

Being in Toast feels a bit like being in a huge soufflé or one of those dreams of heaven that people have in films. It's worlds apart from White Out – almost literally. The whole café seems to be made up of white walls, sunlight and fresh flowers.

And, as I **glance** around, I notice a strange thing – there's not a single man here, only lots of girls who all look a bit like Melissa, with the faces of pretty but horse-like angels, thick shiny hair and big bones. Weird.

Melissa orders a pot of jasmine tea and two pretty lilac **cupcakes** from a woman behind the counter who **resembles** a cross between Princess Diana and My Little Pony. Then we take our order back to our seats, sit at our sunny table and I think in German, dreamily: *Hier ist die Welt noch in Ordnung.*

Except it's not, of course. I feel like half of me is sitting here in London but the other half of me is back in Berlin, with someone else. I'm … torn. The news about Amanda was exciting, of course, and it did take my mind off things

---

✦✦✦ to be s. b.'s cup of tea – jmds. Sache sein ✦✦✦ wicked – genial ✦✦✦ enamel – Zahnschmelz ✦✦✦ to glance – schauen ✦✦✦ cupcake – *muffinähnlicher Kuchen* ✦✦✦ to resemble – ähneln ✦✦✦

for a moment but I'm still uneasy. I'd love to try and talk to Melissa but I don't really know her well enough. And she's so totally, perfectly together Melissa. She wouldn't understand anything about being as schizophrenic as I feel right now.

Melissa doesn't even really ask about my summer holidays. I'm realising now, as she reaches into her handbag, that she has other hot news that she's obviously dying to tell me.

She takes an envelope from her bag and **slides** it over the table to me, looking around the room suspiciously at all the mirror-image reflections of herself as she does so. You'd think the envelope was full of microfilm of top-

+++ to slide – schieben +++

secret weapons or something. "I haven't told Josh yet," she whispers. "It was sent to the school and it was waiting for me when I arrived yesterday."

I haven't opened the envelope and I don't know what "it" is yet but I think I can probably guess. "It" must be something from Olga Petrova, our ex-roommate and Melissa's ex-best friend. Josh is Melissa's brother and he was crazily in love with Olga.

"It" is open and there's a card inside, one made of thick white paper and covered in real little pink **ribbons**. And there, sure enough, on the front is a picture of Olga, looking frankly amazing in a green dress. She's standing under some orange trees, next to a rather orange skinned boy – Taki. Her boyfriend before she met Josh and now, officially, I repeat, *officially*, her fiancé.

I know it's official because under the photo it says in block capitals: *OFFICIAL INVITATION TO THE WEDDING OF MISS OLGA PETROVINOVICH.* (Olga's real name, it seems) *AND MR KONSTANTIN TAKILAKOMIT* (**aka** Taki). It seems a bit strange to call it "official" to me. Maybe Josh has been sending out "unofficial" invitations to his own wedding with Olga?

"Wow," I say slowly. *Double wow*. The wedding is next summer but still, Olga is only a year older than me. Talk about a child **bride**! Even Britney Spears was older! It seems awful somehow, all wrong.

"Have a look inside," says Melissa **grimly**. She's wor-

✦✦✦ ribbon – Band, Bändel ✦✦✦ aka – alias ✦✦✦ bride – Braut ✦✦✦ grim – grimmig ✦✦✦

ried, I can tell. I open the card and there, under all the details of the location, dress code, the super-posh stores where the wedding lists are, Olga has written: *Won't I make a lovely bride?*

Hmm, is she serious? I wonder how much Olga really wants to get married. I bet she'd rather be here playing hockey in the rain with me. Well, she's only human.

Cupcakes eaten, Olga discussed, nothing said about my own problems: time for Melissa and me to head off back to school. En route, Melissa gets a text. It's from Becks, our other roommate, who was supposed to return today. Tomorrow's Monday, the first day of classes. Everyone's supposed to be here by now. Becks' message says: ***Injured groin** at hockey camp, really **sore**. Doc says come back on Wed xx.*

Hmm, a groin injury. I'm actually jealous. Becks always seems to injure herself in the holidays. And that reminds me: it's hockey season again, isn't it? I hate hockey season. Maybe I could pretend to **strain** my groin on the first day.

When Melissa and me arrive back at the dorm, Sadie's there, lying on her bed looking at *How to Learn to Love Yourself* and **frowning**. I throw my arms round her, like she's been a **hostage** in a Phillipine jungle and I successfully **negotiated** her **release** or something. She looks at me a bit uncertainly. "Surprise," she **mutters** softly.

+++ to injure – verletzen +++ groin – Leiste +++ sore – schmerzhaft +++ to strain – zerren +++ to frown – die Stirn runzeln +++ hostage – Geisel +++ to negotiate – verhandeln +++ release – Freilassung +++ to mutter – murmeln +++

"A brilliant one," I say warmly. "We're totally happy to have you here, aren't we, Melissa?"

Melissa, it seems, is too busy texting **furiously** with Becks about her groin to answer: she just smiles vaguely. It looks like she's forgotten that Sadie's living with us already. Sadie glances at Melissa a little sadly: "You're all totally happy *not* to have Amanda in here any more, you mean. But that's cool. I was sick of the old dorm anyway and when Miss Shaw called, it just seemed like the perfect chance for a change of scene."

Just between you and me, the **rumour** was that Sadie was being bullied a bit in her old dorm. Chalk Farm's not exactly the Bronx but still, girls can be cruel. Rich girls can be crueller.

I look over again at what is now Sadie's part of Casa 3B. Sadie hasn't exactly made herself at home yet. Whereas Amanda was the queen of **excess**, Sadie couldn't be any more minimalist. She's only put one photo up: of a country house. There are no people in the picture at all. I don't think it's even Sadie's house, as Sadie's parents live in London. If Sadie went missing and the police came here looking for clues to her personality and lifestyle, they wouldn't find a thing. It's like I'm now living with Erika Mustermann.

You could say the same of me, too, of course. Even though I'm crazy about photography, for instance, I haven't actually got many of my photos up. I really should

---

+++ furious – wütend +++ rumour – Gerücht +++ excess – Übertreibung +++

change that. I always hated having personal things around when Amanda was here. Now she's gone, I can relax a bit. I should really put a picture of Sam up at least.

I look at the photos that I do already have sitting next to my bed, the ones I left there over the holidays. There's one of my parents, quite a boring one taken on our ancient, **filthy** old Ikea sofa at home; one of my brother Max, smiling next to our neighbour's dog and one of … Merle, Betti and me … I freeze … and some other people I don't want to tell you about, that I took last summer. We're standing near the Orankesee in Berlin.

The Orankesee. The Orankesee. The Orankesee. There seems to be a strange echo here, or something. *I'm a terrible person. I'm a terrible person. I'm a terrible person. See what I mean? See what I mean …*

+++ filthy – schmutzig +++

Herman the German

And then, it's Monday and life for this terrible person at Chalk Farm starts again properly. We're in a new **form** now at Chalk Farm, the fourth, but nothing has changed really, except for the fact that we have an even heavier timetable.

One nice change, actually: with no Miss Bardwell around, Miss Shaw, our art teacher, is to take us for registration in the mornings instead. I love Miss Shaw. She's **unique** in our house, Kensington: she's young and hip and totally **rocks**. She really helped me a lot with my photography last term. Even more importantly, she's wearing a purple **batwing dress** from Top Shop that I happen to know was totally sold out in stores and online in two days, fashion fans.

Miss Shaw smiles at me as I come in but it's clear that she has a bad case of "First Day of Term Stress" and she runs through all our names at top speed. The whole school has assembly after this and she must be in a hurry to get there: "I have to rush off this morning, girls," she

---

✦✦✦ form – Klassenstufe ✦✦✦ unique – einzigartig ✦✦✦ to rock – *hier:* ein super Typ sein ✦✦✦ batwing dress – weit geschnittenes, fließendes Kleid ✦✦✦

says. "See you in the main hall in 15 minutes." And – whoosh – off she flies, in her brilliant batwing dress.

I'm just about to turn and say something about her dress to Melissa, who's sitting behind me, when I can't help it – I glance to the back of the room and see Laurie and Amanda, giggling at something. It's Amanda's Black-Berry. It should be shut away in her locker now, of course, but I suppose she doesn't care. She's above the Chalk Farm law, she thinks. She's a **goddess**, she thinks. Then I hear Amanda call, "Oh Sadie, dear, why don't you come and see this?"

Sadie's sitting next to me. "Ignore her," I mutter but Sadie doesn't hear me. Sadie doesn't have much experience with Amanda. She actually goes over to her, like a child going over to get "sweeties" from a nasty stranger.

Amanda points at the little BlackBerry screen and Sadie stares at it with her mouth open, as though it were a light **sabre** or something. She's so naïve. She actually looks sort of hopeful, like she's really expecting Amanda to have sent her good wishes or something. Then she reads whatever's on the screen and her face changes.

I don't have to read it. I'm sure it's something totally nasty or **revolting** written about Sadie on Amanda's MySpace or Twitter page. I can't help it – I see red. I remember only too well what it felt like to have Ed Stanton blogging horrible things about me. I'm not going to let Amanda start BlackBerry bullying everyone.

Bah. I turn around and really face Amanda. It's the first

+++ goddess – Göttin +++ sabre – Säbel +++ revolting – abscheulich

time I've seen her in nearly two months. I wish I could say that she looks awful but tragically, life's never that kind. Amanda never looks awful. She's wearing her brand new holiday **tan** and her skin looks fresh and brown and **crispy**, rather like she's a *Bratente* straight out of the oven or Dieter Bohlen just off the plane from Majorca. Personally, I'd love to put her back in the oven, or back on the plane. Or in the oven *on* the plane, and the plane has no pilot … My imagination is off again.

Amanda's looking at me **blankly**, rather as though we've never been introduced, which is a bit weird, considering that we shared the same air for *months*. Then she smiles, as though she's just realised who I am.

"Why, it's Herman the German! I'm surprised to see *you* back here. I didn't think you'd be able to afford another year. Someone told me the Flying Scotsman had to leave St Dougan's. Someone told me his dad is such a loser he couldn't pay the fees any more."

"Who told you all that – the voices in your head?" I say. Too loud. Amanda rolls her eyes: the left one, a bit bigger than her right one, takes slightly longer to roll – Cyclops! Yeah!

I'm on my feet, suddenly. I can feel my hand forming a **fist**. I wouldn't really punch her, of course. Not in front of **witnesses**.

The whole class is watching me now, I realise. I pass Sadie and she says nervously, "Emily, just take it easy."

✦✦✦ tan – *hier:* Bräune ✦✦✦ crispy – *hier:* zum Anbeißen ✦✦✦ blank – *hier:* ausdruckslos ✦✦✦ fist – Faust ✦✦✦ witness – Zeuge/Zeugin ✦✦✦

I've no idea what I'm going to do or say until I reach Amanda's desk. She doesn't exactly seem nervous by the time I'm standing in front of her, but she does look **expectant**.

I'd love to take the time to really chat with her, of course. I'd love to really get behind why she's such a bitch. (Theory Number One: Amanda has been a little bit angry with the world since her hockey accident. Theory Number Two: Being nasty is fun for Amanda. It's a hobby.)

I don't, though. Here's what I say. It's **badass** stuff: *"Cyclops, I swear if you give me any **grief** this term, I'll stick that BlackBerry where the sun don't shine. Why don't you get your own life and leave us alone?"*

And then I walk off. I hear Amanda laughing behind me, saying, "Did anyone understand her? That weird German accent, I can never get a word of it ..."

But she got it alright. And she knows I mean it. I won't take another term of Amanda Angst. And I stomp all the way to assembly. *Stomp, stomp, stomp.*

Assembly: if I'm lucky I might get to see my good friends Maudie and Kim, who are in another house, Bloomsbury, of course. Home of the Cool. I look over to where Bloomsbury are sitting and as usual, I feel like a farmer with a field of sand, **gazing** over at my neighbour's really green, **lush** grass. Those Bloomsbury chicks just rock.

I spot my own chicks straight away: even in Blooms-

✦✦✦ expectant – erwartungsvoll ✦✦✦ badass – knallharter Typ ✦✦✦ grief – Schmerz, Kummer ✦✦✦ to gaze – blicken ✦✦✦ lush – satt, üppig

bury, Maudie rocks a little bit louder than anyone else. She's the closest thing Chalk Farm has to a punk, our very own Nina Hagen. Maudie's been telling me about her new haircut all summer and I'm seeing it now for the first time. It's a *Vokuhila*, or a **mullet** as they call it in English, with the sides shaved really, really short. It's awesome. I'd love to have my hair like that but I *know* that I'd just look like Rudi Völler. I've had exactly the same hairstyle – shoulder length, **sloping fringe** – well, not since I was *born* probably, but certainly since I've had hair. I'm not exactly the queen of experimentation.

Kim and Maudie have now seen me and are waving over, **frantically**. Kim looks unchanged, which is good, in her case. She's still **drop-dead** pretty, blonde, petite, a little prima ballerina in waiting. Oh, it's **agony**! I'd love to go over to them but I have to stay with my house until assembly is over.

If I survive that long: I'm not sure I can stand sitting through our headmistress Mrs Randall saying *exactly* what she said to us last year, in what looks like *exactly* the same outfit that she wore last year. I **dig** my fingernails into my hand for most of her speech.

When Mrs Randall's finally finished and we've "sung" the Chalk Farm school song – I still don't know the words or the **tune**, so I can't even **hum** it – she introduces our new Latin teacher, a pleasant, hippyish-looking woman

---

+++ mullet – *hier:* Fußballerfrisur +++ sloping fringe – schräger Pony *(Haare)* +++ frantic – heftig, wild +++ drop-dead – wahnsinnig +++ agony – Qual +++ to dig – graben, *hier:* pressen +++ tune – Melodie +++ to hum – summen +++

named Dr Morgan. Mrs Randall says those magical seven words again: *Miss Bardwell will return in six weeks*. I glance over at Cyclops, who just frowns. She was Miss Bardwell's pet and she misses her, like the deserts miss the rain.

Finally – finally! – Mrs Randall cries: "Now girls – off to lessons! Study hard!" and we all nod. And then I rush over to Maudie and Kim: *my girls!* I feel quite emotional seeing them again. Getting to know the two of them was the first thing that made life in London great. They're even more important, of course, now that Sam is gone. And I really need to tell them what happened over summer. I need them to help me make my two 50 percents **equal** 100% again.

+++ to equal – ergeben, gleichen +++

"Ladies!" I shout and Maudie gives me that funny rappers' fist **bump**, like we were Eminem and ... someone else. Then Kim kisses me softly and says quietly, "We've got so much catching up to do." We can't do it now, of course. We've got just enough time to make a date for later. I hear Miss Shaw shout, "*Emily! Latin! You're going the wrong way!*" and I say quickly, "White Out tonight at eight?" Oooh, it's so good to be back! To be **hanging tough** with my Chalk Farm **homies** again.

But my homies aren't that interested in hanging tough, it seems. Instead of **eagerly** agreeing to meet me at eight, Maudie's face falls. Kim's face falls. And it's only then I really understand that Sam not being around isn't going to be the only change in London this year.

Maudie can't do White Out at eight tonight because she has a cinema date at 7.30 pm with Matt, which isn't really a big surprise. What *is* a surprise, however, is that Kim has a date tonight, too!

Oh, that Kim's a real **private** dancer! We texted and mailed a lot over the summer holidays and she never said a *word* to me about having met a boy. She looks embarrassed. "We've just started seeing each other," she mutters. Kim's a dance freak, so it makes sense that her new **beau** is someone she quickstepped into at dance school. His name isn't Christina or Madonna, it seems, but Jonathan.

Kim is **blushing** a bit: "I've been learning the Tango,

+++ bump – leichter Schlag +++ to hang tough – *hier:* zusammen sein +++ homie – Kumpel +++ eager – eifrig +++ private – *hier:* zurückhaltend +++ beau – Verehrer +++ to blush – rot werden +++

did I tell you? Well, Jonathan was the only guy in our group. He's a bit older and he goes to school in Notting Hill. He's nice, a bit shy. He's tall ..." Her voice **tails off**. She now has a huge smile on her face.

"That's great," I say enthusiastically. I really am happy for Maudie and Kim, honestly. They are great friends and beautiful people and they deserve to be loved up and have nice boyfriends. It's their turn. I realise that I spent too much time last year acting like I was Venus, Goddess of Love and not nearly enough time with them.

No problem. "Let's try and **hook up** at the end of the week?" Surely that will be OK. Surely.

But Maudie just looks embarrassed again. She seems to be keeping every night this week "free" for Matt and they have "plans" for the weekend. She could, she thinks, *definitely maybe* meet me between 3 pm and 4.32 pm on Sunday afternoon, though, when Matt has band practice. "The Kitty Gagarins are **auditioning** a new drummer," she says happily, "and ... oh! I'm sorry."

Hmm, that *was* a bit of a tactless comment about the new drummer, wasn't it? Or am I being too sensitive?? And Sunday?? That's *six days* away! I won't make it till then! Who can I talk to? I'll explode! All over the school!

Maudie still looks a bit guilty but says brightly, "So Sunday it is then! Brilliant! I can't wait to hear more about ... Berlin. And Scotland. How *is* Sam? Sorry about talking about the audition for the new drummer before."

+++ to tail off – *hier:* versagen +++ to hook up – sich treffen +++ to audition s. b. – jmdn. vorspielen lassen +++

"No problem," I mumble. Sam's not dead or anything. It *is* hard to imagine someone else taking his place in the Kitty Gagarins, though. They'll never get anyone as good as him, that's clear!

I haven't answered Maudie's question. She looks at me **quizzically**. "Emily? How is Sam?"

"Good," I squeak. God, I can't even answer a question that easy without sounding guilty. *Orankesee, Orankesee.* Oh, I can't believe I'll have to wait so long to try and talk to someone about *not feeling 100%*.

+++ quizzical – belustigt +++

Cracking up

Oh well. I suppose I'll just have to grin and **bear** it … Sunday. It's not that long. It looks generally like I'll be spending all my evenings from now on trying to phone Maudie and Kim's Personal Assistants to book **appointments** with them.

Or **staying in** a lot, actually doing my homework. At least my grandmother, Her Royal Richness the Queen Mother, will be pleased. She called me today, apparently, when I was in the computer room and left a message for me. *Call your grandmother,* said the message. *Says she has something important to tell you.* But I know Grandma: the "something important" will probably be that she broke one of her 18 matching **Wedgewood** egg cups. Plus, she'll be **nagging** me to go and see her at her house, The Grange and I don't want to fix a date to go there yet.

What I do want to do is phone Sam. We've been texting and e-mailing and Facebooking and goodness knows what else ever since I left Scotland, but we haven't

+++ to crack up – durchdrehen +++ to bear – ertragen +++ appointment – Termin +++ to stay in – zu Hause bleiben +++ Wedgewood – Porzellanmarke +++ to nag – nerven +++

actually spoken to each other for ages. We've **vowed** that we won't ring each other too often and will try to save every penny instead for travelling but I can't **resist** it. I call Sam at his mum's and he rings me back at the school phone box. It means everyone will be able to hear me, but I don't care. I just want to hear Sam's voice.

Both Sam and his voice are actually quite chatty tonight, talking pretty much non-stop about his new life. The Scottish schools started a bit earlier so Sam's now been at his new high school for nearly a month. It sounds like he's doing amazingly well. He's joined the football team and he's got a "contact" to a band he might be able to drum with. He's hooked up again with a lot of his old friends from primary school. He's enjoying helping out at the computer shop. He sounds very happy, which I'm **thrilled** about, naturally. I just wish I had something a bit more interesting to tell him about my life. I can't think of anything exciting to tell him at all.

And then things get complicated: Sam and me try and plan our next meeting. It's supposed to be already planned, of course. We've allowed ourselves a couple of weeks to "**settle in**" and Sam is to come down here in two weeks, on the second weekend of term. I'm counting the minutes.

But Sam's now telling me that he can't make it. He's got problems with two of the weekends we'd planned for him to come down. Count them – two of them! We'll have to totally re-write Operation Long Distance Love! It turns

+++ to vow – schwören +++ to resist – widerstehen +++ thrilled – begeistert +++ to settle in – sich einleben +++

out that on one of the weekends he'd wanted to come, he'll now have to do an extra **shift** in the computer shop – for reasons that I don't completely understand but which seem to involve the owner of the shop's cat. "I need the job, Emily, and I can't let them down."

The other thing that will stop Sam coming here *like he promised* is even more serious: Alan will have to go to hospital for a week, for a small operation that he's been keeping very quiet. "So, sorry, but I want to be around that weekend that he's still in hospital. My brothers are really worried."

"I'll come up to Scotland and help out," I say a bit weakly and Sam **sighs**, "Emily, it's just not really the time.

+++ shift – Schicht +++ to sigh – seufzen +++

It would be a waste of money. Just come when we planned – the week after. Have you booked it? We'll just have to **juggle** things, OK? It's **no big deal**."

"*Ermm, no,*" I say. I had actually wanted to talk to Sam about that: it's Kim's birthday the weekend I'm supposed to be in Scotland! She's been telling me for ages to keep it free but I'm such a **birdbrain** that I forgot. It's (almost) the only date in my diary that's interesting! We're all going to go out for a pizza! I *can't* miss that.

"But you can come down here that weekend instead," I say, **wearily**. "Kim would love to see you ... and Matt and Maudie. It would be like old times." And Sam just says in an **annoyed** voice, "I have to work on that Saturday morning, remember? You *know* that. It was hard enough to make a schedule, without you **messing around** with it!"

Messing around with it! Sam's the one who's just cancelled two of the weekends we'd planned! Operation Long Distance Love has barely even started and already it's clear that it really, totally isn't working. We were so **confident** and yet things seem so difficult already. I miss Sam, I really do. But his life seems so full in Scotland, I'm already starting to wonder – does he actually miss me?

Sam then says a bit **grumpily**, "Fine. I'll come down the weekend after Kim's birthday? That OK?"

Oh brother ... not that weekend ... We weren't supposed to meet that week!

+++ to juggle – *hier:* unter einen Hut bringen +++ no big deal – keine große Sache +++ birdbrain – Spatzenhirn +++ weary – lustlos +++ annoyed – verärgert +++ to mess around with s. th. – an etw. herumpfuschen +++ confident – zuversichtlich +++ grumpy – mürrisch +++

"No," I say slowly. "No, can't do that one either." I feel sick. I've just got one word written across the weekend that Sam's just mentioned. It's the only word I've actually got in written in my diary, tragically, apart from *Kim's birthday!!!*

There's a silence at the other end of the line. "And you can't do that weekend because …?"

"Because … I've got someone visiting from Berlin," I mutter.

And that's all I say. Sam's furious with me, I can tell. I don't want to talk about my visitor from Berlin, so he gets all grumpy and then I get all grumpy and we hang up on each other.

It already feels like everything's going wrong. I'm going to crack up, I swear.

It's time to call 112, or 999, as it is here. My emergency service: Maudie, the person I'm closest to in London. Amazingly, I manage to contact her straight away but she instantly starts telling me how sorry she is and listing her dates with Matt. She can definitely, probably still "give me a little tiny bit of time on Sunday afternoon …" I interrupt and say, "*Maudie, it's important. I'm going a bit crazy about something …*" My voice shakes and Maudie says immediately, "No problem. Tonight? Shall I tell Kim?"

I say no, though I'm not really sure why. It just seems easier to **confess** everything to one person than two. *Unter vier Augen* and all that.

+++ to confess – beichten +++

It's Thursday when I'm due to meet Maudie and it's a horrible one. A major storm blows in over London that afternoon. It's quite dramatic and lifts everyone's **mood** when we're in English **Lit** with Mr Benn, even mine. I've just handed in to him what I know is a terrible "What I did in the summer" essay. Awful. All I wrote about was one art gallery that I went to in Edinburgh, like I camped there for six weeks. Talk about not answering the question.

Mr Benn sighs as he flicks through my essay. "I didn't want just a list of paintings Emily," he says. "You were supposed to give an overview of your holiday and what you learned from it." He looks outside at the storm. "I don't think I have to tell you girls that you should stay indoors this evening. There's a weather warning, apparently." And, off he goes, sighing again.

Hmmm, that means that I won't be able to meet Maudie at White Out as we'd planned. We **reschedule**: Maudie will come to dorm 3B. Becks and Melissa will be in the **common room**, watching *Dirty Dancing 2* on television, they've already told me. And Sadie almost certainly won't be in the dorm. She never seems to spend any time there.

Maudie arrives just after eight, carrying a big bag of chocolate drops. We both sit on my bed for a while and watch the rain batter down outside. I make a joke: *"Maybe the hockey **pitch** will get washed away!"* Maudie

---

✦✦✦ mood – Stimmung ✦✦✦ Lit = Literature ✦✦✦ to reschedule – umplanen ✦✦✦ common room – Aufenthaltsraum ✦✦✦ pitch – Feld

laughs politely but she's obviously desperate to hear what she's **sacrificed** an evening with Matt for.

I'm actually too nervous to talk about what's been **bothering** me first, so Maudie starts, chatting a bit about Matt, of course: "I'm sorry I've been so busy with him but I never thought I'd meet a boy like him here … totally easy going, funny." She **hesitates**. "I was jealous of you and Sam last term, you know. You always seemed so happy together."

"We were," I say, **gloomily**, putting three chocolate drops in my mouth at once. "We were."

Maudie looks a bit surprised. "You still *are*, aren't you? I know the distance makes things complicated. But you and Sam are rock steady." She grins encouragingly. "You can do it. You can totally trust him, I'm sure of it. Is that what this is about? You don't trust Sam?"

"I'm not sure that I trust myself," I mutter. Maudie doesn't hear me. Her eye's been caught by a photo by my bed. Her face lights up. "Hey! Betti and Merle, that's a good one of them."

Maudie's spotted the picture I took at the Orankesee this year. The one I didn't totally want to talk about before, remember? The one I'm going to have to talk about now. It's time.

Maudie's still smiling at the photo. She met Betti and Merle when they came here to London at Easter, of course. The three of them got on like a house on fire.

✦✦✦ to sacrifice – opfern ✦✦✦ to bother – *hier:* beschäftigen ✦✦✦
to hesitate – zögern ✦✦✦ gloomy – bedrückt ✦✦✦

"Was that taken this summer? You didn't say very much about how it was in Berlin this summer. Oh, is that Betti's new boyfriend … the **Goth**? Oh, wow! He looks cool. Who are the other two boys?"

Time to open up. I start to give Maudie the whole story. At least the missing 50% of it.

✦✦✦ Goth – Grufti ✦✦✦

The other 50%

The photo taken at the Orankesee, as you might have worked out by now, has six people in it – three boys and three girls. The photo also basically marks the **dividing line** of my holiday in Berlin. Before this picture was taken, even minutes before, the holiday was going well. Too well, I now see.

Just before the photo was taken, I had been back in Berlin for nearly three weeks doing what I always did: seeing Betti and Merle, hanging out in Mondschein – my favourite café in the world before White Out – drinking *Eiskaffee* and **catching up** on all the **gossip**. I felt at home again really quickly, surprisingly quickly. The only slightly weird thing that took a little bit of time to get used to was "LC" being around a lot – Lars-Christoph, Betti's new beau. "The Goth", as Maudie called him. He's lovely, in fact. He looks scary – with his **jet black** hair and leather overalls – but is a **pussycat**. He **worships** Betti and they are very sweet together. So, life in Berlin was good, to begin with.

+++ dividing line – Trennlinie +++ to catch up – aufholen +++ gossip – Tratsch +++ jet black – tiefschwarz +++ pussycat – Schmusekätzchen +++ to worship – anbeten +++

The city was hot, as it often is in July. The day the photo was taken, it was not just hot: it seemed like Prenzlauer Berg, where we live, would **melt** and that we would all be carried away on a **tidal wave** of *geschmolzenes Szeneviertel*. 31 degrees! So we evacuated, heading to the Orankesee, one of our favourite *Freibäder*. There we sat in the shade, eating *Pommes rot-weiß* and *Spaghetti-Eis* (not at the same time). We swam, of course, and laughed at the crazy *sächsische Bademeister* making stupid announcements: *Kevin Barkewitz, deine Mama hat gerade angerufen. Deine Badehose liegt noch zu Hause. Tante Veronika bringt sie in 20 Minuten vorbei*. Then we swam a bit more, lay in the sun some more. Heaven. **Eat your heart out London.**

I was still lying in the sun in heaven, half-listening to LC patiently trying to explain the difference between Thrash Core and True Metal to Betti when Merle suddenly cried out, "Guck mal! Der ist aber heiß, oder?" I **squinted** against the sun to where she was pointing at a tall, **slender** sporty-looking boy, standing in the *Imbiss* queue. Merle was now the only one of us without a boyfriend, of course, so it seemed rude not to at least help her look.

So I rolled over politely and looked. The boy Merle was checking out was quite handsome, with sandy hair and a pleasant face. Good legs. "*Total durchtrainiert*, oder?" groaned Merle. "Und guck …"

✦✦✦ to melt – schmelzen ✦✦✦ tidal wave – Flutwelle ✦✦✦ Eat your heart out London. – Davon kannst du in London nur träumen. ✦✦✦ to squint – blinzeln ✦✦✦ slender – schlank ✦✦✦

I gasped. I knew what she was going to say. The *durchtrainierte* boy Merle's had her eye on had just been joined by an equally *durchtrainierten* friend, also tall and with gorgeous dark hair, deep green eyes ... It's someone we know. Merle said brightly, "Das ist doch Sebastian Junger, oder? Geil, er kann mich jetzt vorstellen."

Sebastian Junger. My own piece of living history. Maudie has no idea who he is. "Sebastian who?" she says, as I reach this part in the story. I've never mentioned him by name to her. He's the boy "German Emily" was crazy about for years in Berlin. Sebastian liked "German Emily" a bit but was never *really* interested in her. He only had eyes for Katharina Müller, our in-house super bitch at Hermann-Hesse-Gymnasium, my school in Berlin. It was only after Katharina found herself a boyfriend and "German Emily" became "English Emily" that Sebastian suddenly found her/me attractive. Typical.

It's odd – I hadn't even **considered** that I might meet Sebastian while I was back in Berlin over the summer. I hadn't really thought about him at all for a while. There had been a time when, I'll admit it, things were bad with Sam and Sebastian and me had *sort of* cyber-flirted a bit. But since I sorted things out with Sam, I can honestly say: Sebastian never entered my head.

But at that moment, down by the lake, with the *Bademeister* making another stupid announcement in the background, Sebastian didn't just enter my head; he entered my personal space, running over (fast, he's a good runner) and hugging me. He was surprised to see me, it was clear – *Du hast doch gesagt, du bleibst in London!* – and a bit hurt that I didn't call him to tell him I was in town but, still, it was a friendly meeting.

To Merle's **delight**, Sebastian's *Joggingkumpel*, Peter – the one she had been **drooling over** – also came over to join us sitting on the grass. It was hot, remember, confusingly hot. I was confused and hot, I repeat. It was quite confusingly nice to see hot Sebastian, who lay down next to me and started chatting naturally, like we had never been apart. Like I'd never left and gone to London. Like I

✦✦✦ to consider – über etw. nachdenken ✦✦✦ delight – Freude ✦✦✦
to drool over – in Verzückung geraten über ✦✦✦

was still sitting behind him in Herr Eisenhardt's *Englisch* class and admiring the back of his neck twice a week.

Anyway, in all the heat and confusion; the following things happened that afternoon. Merle flirted openly with Peter and insisted that I take a photo of the six of us using a self-timer, the three girls and three boys. The three couples. Except we're not, of course. Then we all hung out some more. Merle tried to get Peter's *Handynummer* and **failed**. Merle went into a bad mood. I went in the water a bit with Sebastian, messing around, splashing each other. Just a bit of harmless, platonic fun, naturally. Betti, I did notice, was staring at me in a really strange way.

Finally, before we knew it, the crazy *sächsische Bademeister* was announcing that the *Freibad* would close in ten minutes and everyone was hurrying to get their things together. And that's when Sebastian leant over and whispered to me, "Wollen wir vielleicht noch woanders hingehen? Würde so gerne ein paar Sachen mit dir besprechen."

The 50% of me that is British, of course, just wanted to say, *No thanks, it's been fun but I really must get home.* I'm not totally stupid. Betti was giving me warning looks for a reason: Sebastian had been really, really flirty with me all afternoon. I shouldn't therefore have been interested at all in what Sebastian wanted to talk to me about. But the 50% of me that's German locked the British half of me in a cellar somewhere and said, "Okay, wohin denn?"

+++ to fail – scheitern +++

Back in London, the **suspense** is killing Maudie. She's getting impatient with my atmospheric *Krimi*-style storytelling **approach**. You know, let your reader sweat a bit, make them desperate to know What Happened Next. "OK, OK, just get on with it!" she yelps." Tell me what you did with this Sebastian guy! Are there any chocs left?"

So I tell Maudie, as quickly and as calmly as I can, what happened with "this Sebastian guy". How we managed to meet up secretly; how easy it was. All six of us left the *Freibad* together and got the tram back to Prenzlauer Berg. Although I was actually sitting in front of him, Sebastian then sent me a text in the tram: *Mauerpark?!*

I didn't say anything about the text to Merle or Betti. Betti was going back to LC's place anyway to watch, guess what? Why, *Herr der Ringe*, for the eight millionth time. Merle was obviously still hoping that Peter would ask her out but when he announced that he was going for a run, she finally gave up, sighing, "Ich gehe doch nach Hause. Mutti wollte eigentlich Rouladen machen. Vielleicht sind noch ein paar übrig." I nodded, in a way that I suppose could have suggested that I was also going to go home and look for cold *Rouladen*. Sebastian said nothing. He just looked out of the window smiling, rather as though he were looking forward to something. And I don't mean Mama's *Rinderroulade*.

We all got off at Eberswalderstraße and went our separate ways, Betti and LC, love's young Gothic dream, hand in hand, Merle looking **miserably** at Peter, who

✦✦✦ suspense – Spannung ✦✦✦ approach – Ansatz ✦✦✦ miserable – unglücklich ✦✦✦

jogged off as fast as **greased lightning**. And though Sebastian's way and mine started off as separate, they soon ended up, mysteriously, crossing again about five minutes later. We then walked the short distance to Mauerpark together. I called my parents on the way and told them I would be home by ten. Then I switched my phone off.

"… in case Sam called you!" says Maudie, looking shocked. "Emily! It sounds a bit … like you planned all this quite carefully."

But I didn't. I didn't plan anything. I was excited, to be out on a hot summer's night, with a handsome boy, I admit. It didn't really feel like I was doing anything wrong, though. I wasn't. I was just having a quiet chat with an old school friend. An old school friend that I was once madly in love with. Simple.

Mauerpark is, surprise, surprise, a park where the Wall – yes, *that* Wall, I tell Maudie – once stood. It's a really popular place to sit in summer. I describe the whole scene to Maudie: what everyone is doing around us, for instance. There are people playing bongos. Lots of people spraying graffiti on a wall – no, not that Wall! – at the top of a small hill where young Berliners like to **gather**. Yes, really. This is where the city of Berlin seems to have personally allowed graffiti *Azubis* to train. The air is heavy with the smell of spray paint. It's not really romantic. It's not the Sacré Coeur by night or anything.

Maudie, as I said before, doesn't want me to paint her a picture of our **urban setting**. She says, a bit impatiently,

+++ greased lightning – geölter Blitz +++ to gather – sich treffen +++ urban setting – Stadtkulisse +++

"I get the idea – but what did Sebastian actually want to talk about with you?"

I stare at Maudie. "It was awful," I mutter. "It was the most tragic conversation I've ever had *in my whole entire life.*"

It was the conversation we all have had in our heads at some point, *all of us.* You know the one, the conversation where the boy you love but who doesn't love you back tells you that, in fact: *SURPRISE! He was wrong! He was blind! It was all just a big mistake and you, YES YOU! are the real love of his life.*

I explain to Maudie about Katharina Müller and Maudie sighs. "Boys love those bitchy girls, don't they?"

She's thinking of Rob and Cyclops, of course. "Is that what Sebastian told you? He told you that he wants you now?" She **whistles**. "Emily Hausmann, you are quite the boy magnet, eh? They**'re all into you**."

"Ha, ha," I mumble flatly. There's a silence, then I manage to defend myself. A bit: "I told Sebastian about Sam and how I feel about him. I was totally straight with him about everything."

Maudie's face says: *Is that all?*

"That's not quite all," I tell Maudie slowly. "Just then this bongo player started to …"

"I DON'T CARE ABOUT THE BONGOS!" shouts Maudie. "*Was that it?*"

✦✦✦ to whistle – pfeifen ✦✦✦ to be into s. b. – auf jmdn. stehen ✦✦✦

Man, it's like being **interrogated** by an angry Rottweiler. I whisper, miserably, "Well, then Sebastian started telling me how desperate he was to see London ..."

Maudie interrupts: "You said no, right? Please tell me you didn't invite him to come here!" She puts her head in her hands. She's not happy. It's clear why: she likes Sam, of course, and she *hates* two-timers: the Ed Stanton effect.

I shrug my shoulders and try to look innocent: "I didn't invite him. He invited himself. Kept telling me how much he'd like to come and how terrible his grades for English had been ... really need to improve it *blah blah*. I couldn't say no."

Maudie gasps. "So when is he coming?"

"In three weeks," I say, miserably. It's crazy. I haven't told anyone: *Sebastian Junger is coming here to visit me.* I haven't even told Betti and Merle and I notice they haven't mentioned it, which means that Sebastian hasn't told them either. I'm sure him keeping it secret is a bad sign. I'm sure that confirms that he's thinking of it as a secret romantic meeting and not a *Sprachreise*.

I'm close to tears now. "I've just been worrying and worrying about it for ages. I love Sam but I can't help it: I still like Sebastian, too. A lot. It's been my horrible, awful secret for so long."

Maudie has raised her head from her hands now and is looking more **sympathetic**. She takes control. "OK, let's worry about him coming here in a moment. But that's all

+++ to interrogate – verhören +++ sympathetic – mitfühlend +++

you have to tell me, right … you didn't *do* anything with him?"

"No," I say quietly. "I mean, we did sort of roll around in the grass a bit but … you know. Nothing really."

"*Rolling around in the grass*," repeats Maudie. The kindness has gone from her face again. "Kissing????"

"No! He **tickled** me a bit and so I tickled him back" – Maudie looks **stern** – "and then, a bit of play fighting happened. But no kissing," I finish weakly. Maudie rolls her eyes: "And did you, like, want to kiss him? Did you think about it?"

"*No*," I say to Maudie, though that is only half-true. Only 50% true. That's what I can't really explain to Maudie right now. This is the part that Maudie probably wouldn't understand.

It has to do with me and who I am. I've always been English and German, I've always thought and spoken in both languages. So I have always had two identities and there have always been two Emilys. Everyone is so jealous when I tell them I'm *zweisprachig*/bilingual. It is great, no question. It opens all kinds of doors and saves on all kinds of homework. It is a **gift**. But there is a downside: you're always a bit schizophrenic. Life is all a bit *doppeltes Lottchen*.

Emily *Nummer eins*, you see, the German one, is a bit different from Emily Number Two, English girl. She's a Berliner, so she's slightly rougher and tougher, more

---

✦✦✦ to tickle – kitzeln ✦✦✦ stern – ernst ✦✦✦ gift – Geschenk ✦✦✦

streetwise, somehow, than Emily Number Two, who's posher and a bit more reserved but also funnier. I think I'm funnier in English. And when I take photographs, I also feel more English.

It's a weird and complex thing. *I'm* a weird and complex thing. There's that odd habit of mine of sounding really German when I'm nervous in English, for instance. I mean, what is *that* all about?? I'll probably be working it out in therapy in ten years time and costing myself (or my parents hopefully – it's all their fault!) a **fortune**.

So when it comes to boys, I can only try and explain things this way: English Emily likes being with Sam and German Emily likes being with Sebastian. English Emily likes those rockers! Whereas *deutsche* Emily seems to go for … the boy next door? *Der Athlet von nebenan?* Am I making any sense here?

When I chose to stay here in London last year, I chose to be English Emily. It doesn't mean that German Emily doesn't exist any more. It doesn't mean she doesn't have feelings or desires. But it does mean that I decided to be with Sam. And that's what I say, loud and proud, to Maudie now. "Sam," I say clearly. "I want Sam."

✦✦✦ streetwise – gewieft ✦✦✦ fortune – Vermögen ✦✦✦

Keep calm and carry on

Maudie looks **relieved**. She glances out of the window at the rain – it's still raining, how can that be possible? Don't clouds run out at some time? – and says softly, "Look, Emily, what happened between you and Sebastian wasn't a big deal. But seeing him again here, that's a bit risky, isn't it? I mean, he's probably *not* coming to see Big Ben."

We both burst out laughing, suddenly. It feels good to laugh: I've been so **tense**. Maudie's right, of course. I don't think Sebastian even knows what Big Ben *is*. He'd probably think "Ben" was a *durchtrainierter* long distance runner or something. And Sebastian hasn't exactly bombarded me with a list of museums and art galleries he wants to see, it's true. He seems to be much more worried about things like whether Sam will be around that weekend or not.

Oh, it *is* a nightmare. Why didn't I just tell Sebastian not to come to London after what happened at Mauerpark that night? Nothing happened, of course, but it's clear: *something still could*. Sebastian is really enjoying the game of flirting with me and really wants something to

+++ relieved – erleichtert +++ tense – angespannt +++

happen, that's for sure. He's been e-mailing me all the time – I didn't tell you that either – talking about how much he can't wait to see me again. It's obvious. Letting him come to London is playing with fire.

Maudie, luckily, is my own private emergency service. She can put this fire out! She thinks for a moment, rubbing the **shaven** sides of her *Vokuhila* again. She likes doing that, I've noticed. She says it helps her think.

Then she grins. "Bingo! I've got it. What you need, my girl, is a **chaperone**."

I have to think for a moment to remember what a chaperone actually is. Pictures of old ladies in funny hats jump into my head. I need an old lady in a funny hat? I need … Mrs Randall? The Queen Mother? (*I must call Queen Mother back this week, still haven't managed and must not forget.*)

Maudie looks impatient. "You know, they used to have them years ago. "**Mature**" ladies who helped younger women to preserve their **honour** by going with them on dates! I can do that! I am a few months older than you!"

She smiles, enjoying this now. "I'll drive Sebastian crazy, just you wait! Kim will help out, too. I'll text her and tell her to keep that weekend free. We won't let you sit closer than three metres together. We'll protect you from yourself! Is he staying at Nora's?"

I nod, a bit **numbly**. And before I know it, it's time to

+++ shaven – rasiert +++ chaperone – Anstandsdame +++ mature – reif +++ honour – Ehre +++ numb – benommen +++

forget Operation Long Distance Love for now. I have a new plan to concentrate on: Operation Chaperone. The trick to surviving Sebastian's visit to London is *never to be alone with him.*

After that's all been cleared up, I feel like a new woman. Maudie and me kiss and hug. She's just given me the gifts of both absolution and hope. She's right. It's all no big deal. Nothing happened in Mauerpark. Full stop. Nothing's going to happen in front of Big Ben/the Tower of London/Buckingham Palace, whatever, wherever. Full stop. And once I get Sebastian's visit out of the way and nothing has officially happened, then I can really concentrate on seeing Sam and working out our problems. I can handle that.

So, after Maudie swims back over to Bloomsbury, I'm actually feeling as good as Dr Feelgood in a good mood. It's about 9.30 pm: still no sign of Sadie. Hmm … I'm totally starving, actually. Those chocolates Maudie brought with her were pretty good. She must have got them at the snack machine just along the corridor, right? Maybe it's time for a **refill**. I deserve it. I could murder some more chocolate.

The storm is still **raging** outside as I make my way to snack Mecca, aka the machine at the end of our corridor. I **peer** out of the windows: wow, it looks like that giant **oak tree** in the grounds might come down … and sud-

---

✦✦✦ refill – zweite Portion; Nachschlag ✦✦✦ to rage – wüten ✦✦✦ to peer – spähen ✦✦✦ oak tree – Eiche ✦✦✦

denly – no, it's not the oak tree landing on my head and Maudie saying, *Those were the last words Emily ever wrote* – the lights go out. Totally out! The storm must have caused a **power cut**. I'm plunged into darkness. I hear an "ooh" and lots of squealing from all over the building.

Keep calm and carry on. That's what the Queen Mother tells me they used to say during **WW2**. I'll try. I'd probably be better *not* carrying on for a moment, though. It's probably safer just to wait for the power to go back on here. I'm not a big fan of the dark. I'm not actually scared or anything but still, it's unpleasant. Chalk Farm School is a bit spooky, a bit *schlossgespenstig*, if that word even exists. There is some light coming in through the windows, from the streetlamps on Chalk Farm road so I can sort of see something. Hmm, if only I'd managed to get my chocolate, I could be standing here eating that right now …

Then I hear something. I see something. I'm not alone. There's someone standing at the other end of the corridor. I can't make much out: it's too tall to be one of the girls. It looks like an adult *human being*. One of the **janitors** or a teacher, perhaps. It's a tiny bit odd that the figure hasn't moved or said anything.

"Hello?" I call out nervously.

There's no answer. The figure doesn't move.

"Who's there?" I say more loudly. "It's me, Emily Hausmann. Has there been a power cut?"

✦✦✦ power cut – Stromausfall ✦✦✦ WW2 = World War 2 ✦✦✦ janitor – Hausmeister ✦✦✦

The figure – and by now I'm seriously considering the possibility that it is perhaps not quite human – still says nothing. He or she is as quiet as the **grave**.
Maybe it's Maudie, having a laugh … no it's too tall to be Maudie.
"Hello?" I shout, this time, in a desperate voice. *Hello?????*
Ping! The lights come back on, just as suddenly as they went off. I **heave a** short **sigh of relief** and then peer nervously towards the end of the corridor. Then I let out a huge scream. I was right – the figure isn't quite human!
Miss Bardwell's back.

KAAKOW! A **bolt of lightning** flashes. Miss Bardwell's just standing there, looking like Darth Vader in her strange black cape that some of the teachers here on the Death Star still wear. She looks terrifying. She's not smiling. Her face is totally blank. She doesn't react at all when she sees me.
I can't even believe she's here! Six weeks, Mrs Randall said! It's only the first week of term. But it seems Miss Bardwell's "found herself" early. She looks exactly the same as she did the last time I saw her. The only difference is that she's wearing a big set of what looks like **prayer beads**. She never used to wear any jewellery, apart from a tiny engagement ring, of course, back in the bad old days … or were they good?

✦✦✦ grave – Grab ✦✦✦ to heave a sigh of relief – einen Seufzer der Erleichterung ausstoßen ✦✦✦ bolt of lightning – Blitzschlag ✦✦✦ prayer beads – Gebetsperlen ✦✦✦

"Miss!" I gasp. "I'm sorry. I didn't expect to see you there!" That's true, of course, and much better than saying, *Do you bring news, Lord Vader?*

Miss Bardwell finally reacts, as though a hypnotist somewhere had clicked their fingers. "Ah, Emily. I must apologise. I'm rather nervous of the dark. I just needed a moment to **compose myself** there …"

Miss Bardwell's scared of the dark? That's like a dolphin being scared of water, surely. I thought her people were scared of *sunlight*.

"You're … back, Miss," I say uncertainly. I hope she is, actually. I really hope I'm not imagining this whole scene.

+++ to compose oneself – sich beruhigen +++

Miss Bardwell smiles and there's another roll of thunder, almost as though there was a connection between the two events. (Don't tell me it's a *coincidence* that Miss Bardwell returns during a thunderstorm. The gods are angry.)

She nods stiffly: "I arrived this morning. I had been staying in a **monastery** near Osaka, delightful, so therapeutic … but, well, duty calls. You girls need me, I know that." Miss Bardwell smiles again, sort of. It obviously wasn't very sunny in Japan because she's still the same colour as a Geisha who hasn't left the house in years.

I feel really nervous, actually. All that business with Auntie Nora and Mr Michaels. I'm quite sure I'm going to be made to pay for that somehow. I try to calm myself. A monastery in Japan, that sounds nice, doesn't it? Very **zen**. Lots of people who go off on these retreats come back better people, don't they? Even Darth Vader turned out to be *sort of* a nice guy in the end, didn't he?

Miss Bardwell's staring at me. I'd love to see myself through her eyes: do I have Nora's head attached to my body? "I was a little *surprised* to hear that you are no longer sharing a dorm with Amanda. Yet another personality **clash**, I understand."

Miss Bardwell will *hate* having missed that, of course. She's your classic control freak. She'll *hate* not knowing that Amanda had been moved. She'll think we got rid of Amanda, her pet.

+++ coincidence – Zufall +++ monastery – Kloster +++ zen – *hier:* entspannt +++ clash – Konflikt +++

"Perhaps we should have the beds put on wheels?" I say nervously. Bad joke. Miss Bardwell simply nods again and says **crisply**, "Well, it can't be helped now, I suppose. See you first thing on Monday morning, Emily. I believe you haven't been getting much homework from Dr Morgan. That's something we shall have to change immediately."

I'm not **sensing** a lot of inner peace coming at me, **put it that way**. I don't think Miss Bardwell has changed one tiny bit.

Well, even if Miss Bardwell's not feeling the love, I am. I am full of inner peace, after my great discussion with Maudie. There's just really one tiny thing that would give me total peace of mind right now: if I told Sam how I'm feeling and explain to him about Sebastian coming.

So I decide to write Sam a letter. Yes, you heard me right. I didn't say: write Sam an e-mail or an SMS. I said *letter*. There's a reason for this.

When I imagined being a long distance lover, I'll admit, my image was coloured a bit by my family history. I actually come from a long line of long distance lovers, you see. My parents, for instance: my dad is from East Berlin and he met my mother while she was visiting there from London on a two-week "cultural exchange". (Dad was the son of Mum's tour guide.) Anyway, they fell **head-**

+++ crisp – *hier:* scharf +++ to sense – spüren +++ Put it that way. – Lass es mich so sagen. +++ head-over-heels – Hals über Kopf +++

over-heels in love and managed to keep the relationship going for four years, until the wall fell.

I repeat: *four years.* With the **iron curtain** in the middle and secret policemen reading their letters! With no Internet, no MSN, no Facebook, no texting, not even a reliable phone system. Just good old-fashioned love letters that you waited weeks and weeks for, sometimes. Imagine! I get really frustrated if I want to MSN and Sam's not online, right there and then. I get paranoid and decide that Sam wants to **break up** if he doesn't reply to a text *immediately*.

My father is wrong about a lot of things but he is *totally right* when he tells me that I am the kind of *Weichei* who would have died in a dictatorship. He is *totally right* when he tells me that I have *keine Ahnung, wie das damals war in der DDR.* Thank the stars above I don't. I would totally *hate* to have any real-life experience of living with no phone.

But ... There is a but. I once "**accidentally**" found a bunch of love letters that my parents had sent to each other during their *Brautwerbung.* I then spent three hours "accidentally" reading them. And, of course, hearing all about *what they **longed** to do to each other when they next saw each other* and some stuff was pretty yucky. But there was also something about these letters – so permanent, so exotic, so concrete – that really, really moved me. I mean, how long do you keep even the most roman-

---

✦✦✦ iron curtain – Eiserner Vorhang ✦✦✦ to break up – Schluss machen ✦✦✦ accidentally – zufällig ✦✦✦ to long – sich sehnen ✦✦✦

tic text message? Until you lose your phone, probably, which if you're anything like me, happens every four months. I'm regular as clockwork.

So that's why I decide to write an old-fashioned love letter to Sam now, telling him how I feel about him. I choose some really nice thick paper that I got from the Queen Mother, the kind of stuff that Cleopatra might have written to Anthony on. I'm going to tell Sam everything that's in my heart and my head. Honesty is the best **policy**.

It takes me about two days to actually get round to posting the letter – it's a lot of work writing letters, eh? – but I do it.

Then after some more hard school days it's finally time for some fun. Kim's 15th birthday party, which is a brilliant laugh.

Kim's mum and dad have booked a table at a nice little *trattoria* in Camden. They are lovely, her parents, really relaxed and funny and it's great to meet them. And, almost better, I finally get to meet Jonathan, too, who looks like he's stepped out of a 1930s film. It's hilarious. He's a totally old-school gentleman. He doesn't quite kiss my hand and **bow** deeply when he's introduced to me but he obviously thinks about it. He's exactly the kind of guy who would have gone down with the Titanic, the one who would have said "after you" politely to absolutely everyone pushing in front of him to get on a lifeboat.

+++ policy – Strategie +++ to bow – sich verbeugen +++

There are about ten of us there in total. Maudie and Matt, of course, plus a couple of really cool girls from Bloomsbury and two of Jonathan's friends – a nice mix of people.

I give Kim a DVD of an old production of "Sleeping Beauty" by the Bolshoi Ballet from the 1960s. (Amazon said it was an "essential classic.") Kim seems really pleased and we chat for a little while over our fettucine. She tells me how sorry she is that she's been so busy lately: "Maybe we could go and see a film or something at the weekend?"

The restaurant is loud, of course – it's Italian and full of waiters shouting at each other – so we're speaking loudly, too. Kim seems to have totally forgotten that Sebastian is coming this weekend! I know that Maudie told her everything so I say, in a meaningful and big voice, "I've got an *old school friend from Berlin coming.*"

Kim looks blank for a second. And then – doh! – Maudie's overheard us. She's in a crazy mood tonight, too. She's sitting giggling with Matt and shouts over, "Kim! Operation Chaperone! We have to protect Emily from Sexy Sebastian, remember!"

Kim puts her hand over her mouth. "Ooops! Sorry, Emily – totally forgot!"

It's not Kim that should be putting her hand over her mouth, of course. I could murder Maudie! Matt heard Maudie, too, naturally – I think our waiter's mother in Rome also heard her – and is now looking at me in a really strange way. He's friends with Sam, of course, and they talk a *lot*. Plus there's one other girl here tonight and I'm not certain – but I'm pretty sure I've seen her with Laurie …

Maudie. What a big mouth. She should stick another bruschetta in it and *shut up*.

Operation Chaperone

A week passes, as weeks do. I don't get any reply from Sam. The postal service is slow in Britain. Plus, maybe Sam's written back, which is quite exciting but will take ages.

Anyway, stop all the clocks. It's Friday and "Sexy" Sebastian Junger arrives in London this evening. After classes are over, I go and meet "Auntie" Maudie and "Auntie" Kim, as they keep calling themselves. They think it's really funny, the whole chaperoning business. I'm just a bit worried that it's not just Sebastian that they're going **to drive nuts** this weekend.

We make our way to the airport and wait. And wait some more. Sebastian's flight is late, of course, so I drink too many expensive coffees and get even more nervous.

But finally here he is!

Sebastian's face lights up at first when he spots me. He's carrying his favourite black rucksack and wearing a **denim** jacket, the one that he hardly always wears and which really **suits** him. He walks towards me, holding out his hand.

+++ to drive s. b. nuts – jmdn. verrückt machen +++ denim – Jeans- +++ to suit – *hier:* stehen +++

"Hi," he begins, "ich bin ..." and he **tilts** his head, rather as though he were moving in for a killer kiss. "HI!" booms Maudie suddenly, popping out from behind me. Sebastian jumps a little.

"HI!" echoes Kim, also appearing from behind an advertisement **hoarding**. "You must be SEBASTIAN!"

Sebastian doesn't know where to look. His face is totally puzzled. He glances first at Maudie, then at Kim and finally at me. "Hi," he says uncertainly in English. "You two are friends of Emily?"

"Yes!" yelps Maudie. Oooh, she's loving this just a bit *too* much. I still haven't quite forgiven her for telling everyone in Camden/Western Europe about Sebastian's trip here. She's over-excited again. Maybe I should get her some Ritalin for her birthday.

Maudie giggles. "We're like Emily's *bestest* friends in London. And we'd love to help show you round. First time here? And Emily says you want to practice your English? Brilliant! So no German this weekend – verboten!"

She actually takes poor Sebastian by the arm. "You don't mind if we walk and talk, do you?" Sebastian doesn't know where to look, especially when Kim suddenly appears on his other side. Every time Maudie pauses for breath, Kim fires a question. They're like some kind of crazy talking **seesaw**: "How was the weather in Berlin?" "You love running, I hear?"

Sebastian looks confused. I *think* he's understood

+++ to tilt – neigen +++ hoarding – Plakatwand
+++ seesaw – Wippe +++

everything the girls have said to him but you can tell his brain is **spinning**. He wasn't expecting this. Poor guy. He glances back at me helplessly as Kim and Maudie drag him out of the arrivals hall and towards the bus stop.

Aunties Maudie and Kim take "Seb" – as Maudie now insists on calling him – back to Nora's place, talking at him all the time. Sebastian is certainly getting 100% **immersion** in the English language now. Hey, people pay good money for intensive English courses! He might have arrived here a 3.0 student but he'll leave a 1.3 one!

We stop off quickly at the posh supermarket near Nora's flat to get a couple of things for dinner then we take Seb (see, even I'm calling him that!) to Fitzrovia. When we arrive there, I think I can sense Sebastian waiting for Maudie and Kim to leave. I'm not sure if he's religious; he might even be *praying* for them to go. They are *totally* **exhausting**.

It doesn't happen, though. Maudie and Kim keep talking at Sebastian, telling him all about Nora, how cool she is, how she's working in France at the moment. "Lucky for you, eh?" laughs Kim. "You get to stay in a wicked flat …"

I go off into the kitchen to make – or rather "heat up" – some dinner for us, while Maudie and Kim stay in the living room with their prisoner. I can hear Maudie saying, "Hey Seb! I'm guessing you're more of a Stones than a Beatles guy, am I right?" It seems the girls are going

+++ to spin – sich drehen +++ immersion – Eintauchen +++
exhausting – anstrengend +++

through Nora's enormous vinyl collection, arguing loudly about which album to put on.

While his "bodyguards" are busy, Sebastian obviously sees his chance and escapes into the kitchen. I turn around and there he is! Nora's kitchen is tiny, so it's automatically an intimate moment – it's not possible for Sebastian to stand more than 20 centimetres away from me.

He's so close I can smell him and, boy, even after an afternoon on an aeroplane and London's public transport, he still smells nice. Suddenly we're standing face to face and I'm back in Mauerpark. I feel like I should be hitting a panic button for Maudie and Kim …

Sebastian's obviously scared that his (or are they my?) guards will notice he's gone, so he talks quickly and quietly, glancing nervously over his shoulder: "Ich wollte ganz kurz mit dir reden und fragen, wie es dir so geht … Ich meine, deine Freundinnen sind ganz nett und so. Aber wollen wir nicht ein bisschen Zeit alleine verbringen …?"

"HEYYYY!!" It's Kim, **leaping** between us, like a **referee** in a boxing match. "What are you two up to? Wow, Emily, quiche! That looks brilliant! Sebastian, do you have quiche in Germany? Emily, how do you say quiche in German?"

"Quiche," I say slowly. I'm not sure how long I'm going to be able to **stand** this, actually.

Day One of "Operation Chaperone" is a total success, if you can call having your nerves **chopped** into tiny

---

✦✦✦ to leap – springen ✦✦✦ referee – *hier:* Ringrichter ✦✦✦ to stand – *hier:* aushalten ✦✦✦ to chop – klein schneiden ✦✦✦

pieces by your two best friends and ruining one boy's holiday a "total success". Statistically seen, though, it's all perfect: Sebastian and me were left alone for approximately 1.2 minutes. "An excellent day's work!" sighs Maudie as she and Kim high five each other.

Hmmm. I suppose I should be **grateful** that my best friends are finally spending some time with me! But that night I find myself lying in bed and dreaming about how things would have been if I hadn't told Maudie about Sebastian and what happened in Berlin. Then Maudie and Kim come screaming into my brain on motorcycles, wearing uniforms saying "Thought Police" on them and shouting at me to *stop dreaming about that!* So I do.

One day of Sebastian's visit down, two to go. Saturday we've arranged to pick him up and show him the Houses of Parliament and, guess what, Big Ben. It was Maudie's idea to take him there. She thought it was really, really funny. Ha, ha, ha.

I meet Maudie and Kim outside school and then we head off to Nora's. It's raining. Again. It seems to have done nothing but rain in London this autumn. We've brought umbrellas. Maudie even has a strange-looking purple one with her for Sebastian.

When we ring the buzzer downstairs, Sebastian answers quickly as though he's been waiting for us. He says, a bit desperately, "Bist du alleine? Willst du vielleicht nach oben kommen …?"

+++ grateful – dankbar +++

"Alleine!" says Maudie loudly, leaning in towards the entryphone. "I know what that word means! No German! Come on, get yourself down here. We've got loads of sights to see."

I think I hear Sebastian mutter, "Um Gottes willen." So he is religious! When he comes downstairs, his face when he sees Maudie and Kim is a picture, like one of those Munch paintings of someone screaming. Completely traumatised.

Sebastian Junger – and I don't know him all that well but I'm almost certain of this – is having the worst time of his life here in London with us. He doesn't react to Big Ben or the Houses of Parliament at all: I nearly check his pulse at one point. I try cracking some jokes to lighten things up but he doesn't have the world's best sense of humour, Sebastian. He doesn't even have *Germany's* best sense of humour, I'm realising. Sam would have found my jokes funny, I'm sure.

Armer "Seb" looks so miserable that I finally say **in desperation**, "Hey, why don't we head down to Trainer Universe?" Trainer Universe is London's biggest sport shoes shop and I'm hoping that might cheer Sebastian up. It's also at Trafalgar Square, so it's not far. And, **miracle** of miracles, Sebastian does indeed smile, finally, when I suggest going there. I have a funny feeling it's the best thing that has happened to Sebastian since he came to London. The day is saved.

While Sebastian is checking out running shoes at Trainer Universe, with Maudie and Kim watching him like Secret Service agents in the background, my phone rings. It's Sam! I instantly feel nervous – perhaps he's got my letter?

Sam barely even says hi, he just gets straight to the point: "Cyclops just left a message on my Facebook page. Really charming, asking how I was getting on and saying how sorry she was that we've *broken up*. Oh, and she asked who the *handsome German stranger* was that she'd seen you walking hand in hand with?"

"That's nonsense!" I **splutter**. "Cyclops has never seen him in her life before! She can't know what he looks like!"

+++ in desperation – aus Verzweiflung +++ miracle – Wunder +++ to splutter – herausplatzen +++

Not a very clever response, was it? Sam just laughs. "Nice one." He sounds furious. "Remember I said you could trust me? Well, I meant it. And remember you said I could trust you?"

Sam obviously never got my letter. Man, it's a miracle that the human race has stayed around so long. How did anyone manage to **conduct** a relationship before we had computers and mobile phones? Nightmare.

I can't say anything. Out of the corner of my eye, I see Sebastian holding a pair of blue and yellow running shoes up to me, as if to say: *Diese hier?* I nod helplessly.

"Didn't you get my letter? I wrote you one explaining things ..."

There's a stony silence from Sam. Ooh, that did sound awful, actually. The only reason anyone writes letters these days is, well, to finish a relationship.

More *Funkstille*. I try to fill the dead air: "Sebastian's an old school friend, that's all," I say. I wouldn't believe me, I even sound guilty to my own ears. "Maudie and Kim are here. They've been with us all the time ..." Oh, that sounds suspicious, too.

"And we're meeting Matt later ..." I've no idea if I'm making things better or worse but I can't bear the silence. Meeting Matt – that must be **evidence** that nothing at all is happening with Sebastian.

"I know you're meeting Matt later," says Sam grimly. "He told me. And he also mentioned something about Sexy Sebastian."

+++ to conduct – führen +++ evidence – Beweis +++

Privacy. So **last century**, isn't it? I really do feel like I'm living in that old Police song – you know, *Every Breath You Take. Every Move You Make.* Someone, somewhere, will be watching you.

Here's a quick rundown of what happens after I spoke to Sam: Sebastian buys the blue and yellow trainers. We meet Matt for a pizza and Matt is totally cold to both Sebastian and me. This puts me in a really bad mood that lasts 36 whole hours. We get through one more miserable day together, Sebastian, me and my beloved chaperones. We go to the Tate Modern and no one really says a word to each other all day. Sebastian just stares at his new trainers all day as though he's trying to tell himself that the whole trip hasn't been a total waste of time.

Then, finally, it's over. Sebastian leaves. His face is ecstatic. His face says, *Berlin! Berlin! Ich fahre nach Berlin!* He can't wait to get back. He thanks me and my shadows for the trip then gives me one last funny look before he goes. I can't quite read it: The look either says: *I will never forgive you* or *What did I ever see in you?*

And me? How do I feel when Sebastian leaves? The same way he does – relieved. Relieved that we didn't do anything. And really relieved that I won't have to see Maudie and Kim for a while either! Their boyfriends can keep them!

I'm annoyed, too, of course. I didn't so much as *breathe* near Sebastian and yet Sam still seems to think I'm guilty

+++ last century – *hier:* altmodisch +++

of **cheating on** him. Neither of us has called the other since the horrible conversation in Trainer Universe. Each of us seems to think it's the other's move.

When I get back to school, there's a letter waiting for me. Guess who it's from? Yes, it's from me. It's the letter I "sent" to Sam, which has been returned due to "**insufficient** postage". I shake my fist at the heavens and decide I'll write Sam an e-mail. So much for old-school romance.

+++ to cheat on s. b. – jmdn. betrügen/hintergehen +++ insufficient – nicht ausreichend +++

The sweet Smell of Nepotism

With all my boy problems, I have certainly been **neglecting** my family. My grandma of course, whom – I'm so ashamed! – I still haven't phoned back to find out what was so important! And my aunt Nora. I haven't seen her since I've been back in London. I miss her.

It's not all my fault, of course – Nora has hardly been in town since school started. I'm not even sure when she's back from France but I try her at home one day spontaneously and nearly have a heart attack when she picks the phone up!!

Hurrah! She's "just come in the door", apparently, and tells me straight away that she has something important she wants to discuss with me. What is it with my family and "important things" to discuss at the moment? The difference between Nora and the Queen Mother is, of course, that Nora's idea of something important probably actually *is*.

Nora and me arrange to meet in a Vietnamese restaurant near her home in Fitzrovia the next day. I, being a

+++ nepotism – Vetternwirtschaft +++ to neglect – vernachlässigen +++

tactical genius, calculate that I should arrive 25 minutes after the time we agreed in order to be "punctual" for Nora and we arrive – ha! – at the doorway to the restaurant at *exactly* the same millisecond. Ha! How we laughed!

Once we're inside and **battling** with our **chopsticks**, we talk and talk. Or I talk and talk. Now that I've survived Sebastian's visit and *didn't do anything!* I can tell Nora about Sam and how we're trying to work at staying together and she nods and smiles a bit sadly. I wonder …

Nora and me haven't ever really discussed Mr Michaels. Mr Michaels went off to teach in Uganda, after realising Nora wasn't interested in him. He probably hoped that it would be far enough away from Miss Bardwell. I wonder sometimes – I wonder quite often, actually – whether he and Nora are still **in touch**. There's a tiny part of me that would like to know why she's looking so dreamy as I talk about long distance relationships.

Anyway, Nora gives me some general advice about boys, things like: *Don't be too intense with them! Give Sam a bit of space!* And then I realise that she's bored of talking about boys so we start discussing photography instead. I'm a bit ashamed, actually. I've been so **wrapped up in** my own love life that I've barely touched my camera. But I tell Nora that I'm planning to put together a good portfolio and her face lights up.

+++ to battle – kämpfen +++ chopsticks – Stäbchen +++ to be in touch (with s. b.) – (mit jmdm.) in Kontakt stehen +++ to be wrapped up in – beschäftigt sein mit +++

"That's actually sort of why I brought you here tonight …"

Is it possible to be **spoilt** and have no money at the same time? Because that's what I think I am. My family give me everything, have you noticed? I get my fees paid at a posh school by my kindly Grandmother. I have the universe's coolest, kindest aunt, who has a great flat in London that lies empty a lot and I get to "play" in. And now … What's that? Ah, it's the sweet smell of nepotism once again!

Nora has managed to get me some work experience at her newspaper, *The* **Sentinel**. It's really true. I won't get paid a penny, of course, and it would only be for one afternoon a week but still, it would give me a chance to see a real live newsroom. "You wouldn't get to do that much really," says Nora, frowning "but you'd be in the art department and you'd see how they use computers. You need to know about that. And it will be time sooner or later to get yourself a *digital camera*."

I gasp. Actually, I know it's true. I'm the only person on this planet still working with film. I do love my camera, though I have to say using it hasn't felt *quite* the same since I lost it to Cyclops for a while after a stupid **bet** I made.

Nora smiles. She's got the perfect solution again. She's too good. "Actually, I have a friend who wants to sell his old camera. Not that it's old, it's more or less brand new." She tells me about the camera – it does sound amazing and the price her friend wants is really, really fair. "I could

---

✦✦✦ spoilt – verzogen ✦✦✦ sentinel – Wachposten ✦✦✦ bet – Wette

buy if for you, as an early birthday present," says Nora warmly.

Even I have my **pride**. Suddenly I see Sam, right in front of my eyes, shaking his head. I remember what he said about spoilt kids. Kids who don't know the value of anything because they've never had to work for it. I don't want to be like that.

"I'm interested in the camera but I'll pay for it myself," I say proudly and as Nora protests, I repeat firmly, "*I'll pay for it myself.*" I don't really know how, of course, but finally we agree that Nora will try and work out a payment plan with her friend for the camera. It will cost me nearly all of my pocket money but it will give me a totally professional, **cutting-edge** camera. The future's bright and it's digital.

I feel much better. I have goals, a new camera, something interesting to do. I still need to tell one person before it's official, of course. It shouldn't be too complicated really. I could go to *The Sentinel* for a few hours on a Wednesday afternoon, which is when we have "**Leisure**" at school (i.e. we are supposed to be **attending** a course in one of our hobbies like **chess** or **knitting**. No one ever seems to go.). It's no big deal. It's a great chance for me, any teacher will see that.

It's true that the *any teacher* I have to ask for **permission** is Miss Bardwell, the Chairwoman of the Emily

---

✦✦✦ pride – Stolz ✦✦✦ cutting-edge – supermodern ✦✦✦ leisure – Freizeit ✦✦✦ to attend – besuchen ✦✦✦ chess – Schach ✦✦✦ to knit – stricken ✦✦✦ permission – Erlaubnis ✦✦✦

Hausmann Fan Club. It's true that, just as I guessed, Miss Bardwell hasn't been very zen so far with us since she got back from Japan – we've had so much homework that Sadie really, really cried after our last Latin class. Miss Bardwell also seems to be back **in league with** Amanda. I keep seeing them together, laughing and holding hands … no, OK, not actually holding hands. But they certainly seem to do a lot of laughing about something together.

Positive thinking. Everyone has the potential to change, someone once told me that. But when I go to see Miss Bardwell and tell her about my amazing, brilliant chance of a lifetime, she looks me up and down and plays frantically with her prayer beads.

At first she nods and smiles encouragingly as I tell her about *The Sentinel*. But when I finish talking, Miss Bardwell just says, simply, "The answer is NO." This NO is said loudly, with a smile and a rattle of her beads.

When I ask why the answer is NO, Miss Bardwell does not hesitate. She has at least ten reasons why: it's *against school policy, health and safety rules,* **setting a precedent**. She might as well add: *because I enjoy killing your hopes and dreams stone dead. And because I will never forgive your aunt for destroying my relationship.* Those are the real reasons, I know it.

All the Buddhist chanting in the world will never make Miss Bardwell forgive Nora for ruining her only chance at a love life.

✦✦✦ to be in league with s. b. – hier: sich mit jmdm. verbünden ✦✦✦
to set a precedent – ein Beispiel setzen ✦✦✦

So that's that then. No newspaper. No future. I phone Nora to tell her, trying not to cry and trying not to sound too bitter. Nora says quickly, "Give me five minutes. I'll call you back."

And five minutes later, she does just that. She sounds a bit breathless: "I've **sorted** something else **out** – what about coming in at weekends, if the school won't let you do weekdays? The art department boss, Todd, is a total sweetheart and he's happy to let you help out on Saturdays. No need really even to tell the school, yet."

YEEEAAAHHH!!! "Brilliant," I say. *Brilliant.*

I hang up on Nora and it's only then that I realise: Saturdays? What about Sam? What about keeping my weekends free for him? And how on earth am I going to pay for my new camera *and* budget for trips to Scotland?

I worry about that, of course. I'm also really worried about putting together a decent portfolio in time for *The Sentinel*. Nora said that Todd *would really like to see my work*. "I've told him how talented you are!"

Oh, great, so no **pressure**! I've filled up the photo diary that Nora gave me when I came to London and I'm *quite* proud of it. It's *quite* nice, the kind of thing that I could take for a *Bewerbungsgespräch* with Herrn Putz if I wanted to be his *Azubi*. Herr Putz runs the photo shop downstairs from our flat in Berlin and seems to specialise in badly photo-shopped pictures of sexy girls and big men with bad tattoos showing off their new babies.

✦✦✦ to sort s. th. out – etw. klären ✦✦✦ pressure – Druck ✦✦✦

But I don't want to be *that* kind of photographer. I want to be a proper one, like Auntie Nora, who takes pictures that tell stories and reflect reality. I want to work in journalism. I want to work for people like Todd, the sweetheart.

So I've set myself the project of trying to put together a new portfolio: this time of street life in Camden. Chalk Farm School and its community of spoilt princesses is no reflection of reality, of course, but Camden itself is a crazy place, full of colourful characters, cool people.

I already have some "characters" in mind whom I see around a lot: there are those two old ladies, for instance, who always sit in their wheelchairs outside our school, smoking cigarettes; that man who sells the **potato peelers** down at the Market, the one with the **eye patch** …

So I spend the next day running around Camden with my camera, shooting film after film. I don't tell my camera about the new camera I'll be getting, a bit like I didn't tell Sam about Sebastian. You can really trust me, right?

I'm in Chemistry on Tuesday, writing my e-mail in my head to Sam, which will now have to be a saga. I heard **recently** that there are a trillion pages on the Internet. That number will double by the time I've explained everything that needs explaining to Sam: *Sebastian; why my letter never arrived; The Sentinel at weekends; using my money to buy a camera and not for coach trips.*

✦✦✦ potato peeler – Kartoffelschäler ✦✦✦ eye patch – Augenklappe ✦✦✦ recently – vor Kurzem ✦✦✦

I'm on about the fifteenth page (still in my head) of my e-mail to Sam when a **prefect** from the year above us, a nice looking girl called Satsuko, comes in. She whispers something in the ear of Mr Evans-Brown, our Chemistry teacher, who's unsuccessfully trying to show us how to make soap. "Emily," he says in an irritated sounding voice, "there's someone downstairs in the lobby who wants to talk to you. It's important, apparently."

I can't help it – for a moment I think of Sam, even though I know it can't be. I leave Melissa battling to save our experiment and follow Satsuko. She doesn't know

+++ prefect – Vertrauensschüler/in +++

much else, she tells me as we go downstairs, just that it's a woman who's waiting to see me.

It is all really strange. It's the middle of the school day. I come downstairs into the lobby and there, sitting in a chair, is Nora!

Nora! Brilliant … but … why? My first thought is: oooh, maybe she's **dropping off** my new camera!

Nora's looking at the floor when I first see her and I notice that it takes her a long time to lift her head, even though I'm sure she's heard Satsuko and me come down the stairs. It's just then that I realise this has nothing at all to do with cameras. It's bad news, it must be. I'm scared. What if something is wrong at home? Max, I think suddenly. Something's happened to my little brother Max.

I sit down opposite Nora and she says very calmly, "Emily, it's your grandmother …"

The Queen Mother died in her sleep, sometime early this morning. It was, as they always say it was (and no one can really know) very peaceful. My grandmother's housekeeper found her when she came in to make breakfast.

Nora tells me all this as though she were simply reading aloud one of the stories from her newspaper, about someone she didn't know. "She won't have felt anything. She just slipped away. It's the way she would have wanted to go. No pain, no **fuss**, no …" Nora's voice breaks just a little, "… no kissing goodbye."

She reaches over and takes my hand. "I'm sorry, Emily.

+++ to drop off – vorbeibringen +++ fuss – Aufhebens +++

Your mother asked me to come here and tell you personally. I'm going to take you to my place tonight. It would be for the best, I think. We can talk to your mum from there. She's trying to get flights sorted out from Berlin right now."

Nora sits up very straight. She seems almost totally relaxed, almost. She must be in shock. Me, I can't stop shaking. All I can think is: *I kept meaning to phone her. I haven't spoken to her in weeks and now it's too late. There's no chance to say goodbye.*

"Let's go," says Nora, whispering. "Don't worry about Miss Bardwell. Let's just leave."

I stand up. My legs feel like they are made out of thousands of *Gummibärchen* but I still manage to get upstairs to the dorm quickly to pick up some of my things. There's no one around: everyone in my class is still trying to make soap. How stupid that seems suddenly, how **pointless**.

Alone in the dorm, I grab my **case** from under my bed and throw in ... what? It suddenly hits me that there will be a *funeral*. I'll be going to the Queen Mother's funeral. I need something to wear to that.

I feel ill for a second. I look at my clothes: what should I wear? A black T-shirt? My denim skirt? Then I realise that the best way to show the Queen Mother respect would be to wear what I'm wearing now – my Chalk Farm school uniform. The Queen Mother loved this school.

✦✦✦ pointless – zwecklos ✦✦✦ case – Koffer
✦✦✦ funeral – Beerdigung ✦✦✦

She changed my life by sending me here and now she's gone.

I sit on my bed and, just for four or five minutes, I **weep**. I have to. Then I think of Nora waiting downstairs and how much I *really* don't want either of us to see Miss Bardwell and I close my case.

I grab my purse and my mobile from my locker. I stare hard at my phone. I should call Sam, of course. I *want* to call Sam, somehow. I should let him know about my grandmother. I should probably call Betti and Merle and let them know, too. Oh, and Kim and Maudie ... And ... **I can't help it**, I think for a moment about calling Sebastian. His visit was a disaster but, still, I somehow feel like I should tell him.

I don't call anyone in the end. I can't. It doesn't seem right. I couldn't be bothered to phone my own grandmother for weeks. I was too lazy. It was too much trouble. So I certainly shouldn't be on the phone to my friends now.

I do write two text messages, one in English and one in German. The English one says: *Grandmother died this morning. Going with Nora to Grange. I'll call you x.* I send it to Maudie, Kim, Melissa, Becks and Sam, of course.

In German I write: *Meine Grandma ist heute Morgen eingeschlafen. Ich meld mich.* I send it to Betti, Merle and ... Sebastian. I can't, as I say, help it. Then I switch my phone off, and run back downstairs to Nora.

✦✦✦ to weep – weinen ✦✦✦ I can't help it. – Ich kann nicht anders. ✦✦✦

Who your Friends are

I spend the night at Nora's and what a rotten night it is, too. I can't sleep at all. I wander round the kitchen and the living room, watching TV, crying a bit, watching a bit more TV, crying a bit more.

I don't see anything of Nora until the following morning. She seems to have **slept like a log**. She's positively **jolly** now. She is a bit *too* jolly, more **manic** really – she can't stop talking and is constantly on the phone. Nora has the job of calling all of the Queen Mother's friends – those that are still alive, of course. I don't know how she can do it. I hear her say the same sentence over and over again. *Slipped away in the night. Painless. Yes, the arrangements will be in The Times tomorrow.*

"She was the second last survivor of her year at Chalk Farm School," Nora tells me, looking at a list she seems to have made. "Millie is the only one left from their year. She's your friend's grandmother, isn't she?" Millie is Becks' grandma. It was through Millie that I came to Chalk Farm School **in the first place**, I remember, miserably.

+++ to sleep like a log – wie ein Murmeltier schlafen +++ jolly – munter +++ manic – manisch +++ in the first place – überhaupt erst

I can't help Nora with anything, I just can't. I don't seem to be able to do anything except sit around and cry and wait for my family to arrive from Berlin. Luckily, they've got on a flight more or less immediately.

Nora and me go in her old Citroën to pick them up next day from the airport. All I seem to have done, have you noticed, over the past few months, is arrive at/leave airports. I'm back in the same arrivals hall where I was a few days ago to meet Sebastian. Back when my biggest worry was – oh no! – that a handsome boy might try and kiss me again. Ha!

I get two shocks when the rest of the Hausmann family come through into the arrivals hall. The first one is Mum. I realised she'd be **upset** – I mean, the Queen Mother was, like, her mother – but Mum doesn't just look upset, she looks like she's been hit in the face with the branch of a tree, often, by a lot of people. Her face is totally purple and swollen from crying.

And there's another shock – they've brought Onkel Dieter with them.

I can't believe it! Onkel Dieter from Eisenhüttenstadt! The really odd one with a weird **ginger moustache**. Who wears *Modern Talking* T-shirts with no irony! Who speaks ze really terrible Ingleesh! Onkel Dieter doesn't belong in England! He must be **wanted** for crimes against the English language.

+++ to be upset – erschüttert sein +++ ginger – rotblond +++ moustache – Schnurrbart +++ to be wanted – polizeilich gesucht werden +++

My father knows my feelings about my uncle and, after he's hugged me and asked me how I am, he says quickly, "Dieter war zu Besuch, als wir die Nachricht bekommen haben. Wir dachten, er könnte ein bisschen auf dich und Max aufpassen. Dieter kommt immer prima zurecht mit Max." Dad puts his arm around me but gives me a stern look at the same time: "Wir brauchen gerade Unterstützung. Wie du siehst, ist deine Mama nicht in der Lage, sich um viel zu kümmern, und bei Nora weiß man nie …"

He looks over at my aunt, doubtfully. Nora is hugging my mother. They don't look alike at the best of times, the two sisters, and now, at the worst of times, they look even less alike. You would think my mother had just done twelve rounds with Vladimir Klitschko whereas Nora looks like she's just returned from a refreshing **spa** weekend. I've no idea what's going through Nora's head. Does she feel … anything?

Onkel Dieter is walking towards me now. He has his arm round Max. It's true, of course, he does get on brilliantly with my brother. Max thinks he's hilarious. They communicate on the same level, of course. Lots of **fart** jokes and stuff.

Max. My little brother. I wonder how he feels about losing his grandmother. He's only ten. I suppose he hardly knew her, really. We never saw much of Grandma when we were younger. She never came to Germany *on principle*. You know: *that nasty Luftwaffe.*

Max gives me a hug. "Hi, big sis," he says. "You OK?"

I nod and **ruffle** his hair. Then I nod at Onkel Dieter and shake his hand, a bit stiffly. Dieter says in English, "How a zu?" or something and I say, quickly in German, "Alles in Ordnung." Oh, don't let him speak English here in public! It's *sooo* embarrassing.

"Ve had ze very nice flight," Dieter says cheerfully. He never actually met my grandmother and I think he's just really happy to be getting a free holiday. He's standing too near to me. He always does. He has no antenna for Personal Space. "Sorry for your … wie hieß die noch mal? Beatrice."

I'd almost forgotten that that was the Queen Mother's

+++ spa – *hier:* Wellness +++ fart – Furz +++ to ruffle – zerraufen +++

name. Then I just know what Dieter's going to do next and he does: he pulls a **coin** out from behind his ear. Max shrieks with delight.

There's not enough room in Nora's car for all of us now, as no one had remembered to tell Nora that Dieter was coming, so I **volunteer** "bravely" to take the train back by myself to Surrey. In my heart of hearts, I'm totally relieved, of course, that I won't have to listen to my mother crying and my uncle talking his "Dieter's Denglish" nonsense.

The train journey also gives me time to sit back and reflect in peace on what's happened over the past couple of days. I haven't spoken to any of my friends since I left Chalk Farm School. I haven't even turned my phone on. I should really call Sam at least.

I'm nervous about it, of course. Last time we spoke, we had that awful fight about Sebastian. He probably doesn't care about my grandmother. No. That's right. He won't care.

I switch my phone on. I **punch in** my code and then hold my breath.

I have eleven missed calls. *Eleven*. I only ever had that number once before, that time Betti and Merle saw Sebastian walking down Kastanienallee with Katharina Müller some time ago and kept trying to ring me to tell me the news.

Six calls, count them – six! – are from Sam. One is from

✦✦✦ coin – Münze ✦✦✦ to volunteer – freiwillig tun ✦✦✦ to punch in – eintippen ✦✦✦

Maudie, one is from Kim and one is from a number that it takes me a minute to recognise, then I realise is Melissa.

I go to my mailbox. In the six messages from Sam he sounds really upset, in all of them. *I'm so sorry ... give me a call when you can.* The same message over and over: *Just me again. Are you OK? Phone me back.*

Loads of texts from Betti and Merle, too. No message from Sebastian, I notice.

Next morning and the day of the funeral: I can only think about how I will survive the day. I've never been to a funeral before. My grandfather – yes, Queen Father! – died when I was really small: I don't even remember him. I've no idea how to act today, no game plan.

I get into my school uniform. It takes ages. I can't stop thinking about that first day at Broughton's the uniform shop, buying it with the Queen Mother. Her fighting with Nora non-stop ... ah, good times.

Nora comes to find me, just as I'm remembering her arguing with her mother. "Alright?" she says gently. She has on a smart dark grey trouser suit which is perfect for a funeral and the kind of thing I would love to be wearing.

I nod but, actually, I'm **terrified**. Nora smiles: she's carrying something, I now see. It's a camera. For a moment, I feel a bit shocked. She's not going to take pictures of the funeral, is she??

"I brought your new camera with me," Nora says qui-

+++ to be terrified – große Angst haben +++

etly. "I know now's not really the time but there probably won't *be* a good time over the next couple of days. And Trevor, my friend, the one who's selling it says don't worry about the first payment for now."

I look in the camera case. I don't take it out. I'm going to save that for later.

"Thanks," I whisper to Nora. It's not the time to cry, of course. If I start this early in the day, I'm finished.

When I finally come downstairs in my uniform, Max bursts out laughing. He's never seen me in it before, of course. Onkel Dieter tells me, bizarrely, that I look like I'm in the FDJ. "Sieht ein bisschen aus wie eine Pionieruniform, oder, Sascha?" My father sighs. "Na ja, Dieter, außer dass die Pionieruniform eine ganz andere Farbe hatte, ja, die sehen genauso aus."

When we arrive at the church in the village nearest The Grange, the place is **packed** already. The Queen Mother went to this church every Sunday and everyone, it seems, knew her. Everyone, it seems, liked her. It's really moving to see all these people sitting here for her, looking sad. I can't help it: I wonder how many people would come to my funeral. We wouldn't need a big church to hold it in, put it that way.

And I'm relieved to see that I'm not the only one wearing a Chalk Farm uniform. Becks is here, too! She's come with her grandmother, "Millie", who looks about 108. I'm so happy to see Becks, even though she gives me one of

✦✦✦ packed – brechend voll ✦✦✦

her bone-breaking bear hugs. "I tried to call you this morning to tell you I was coming but your phone was always switched off," she **hisses**. It's true, I haven't had it on today yet. I still can't face it. I have phone guilt.

Becks and her grandmother take their seats next to us in the front row. Becks whispers to me, "I'm not the only one from the school here, of course …" She nods towards the back of the church.

She must mean Miss Bardwell. I turn and there she is, dressed in black – unusual! She probably **hired** her outfit! Ha! She's with Mrs Randall, our headmistress. Mrs Randall seems to have gone for some sort of mad Queen Mother **tribute** hat today. The hat has what looks like – but can't be, of course, it just can't – the Parthenon in Athens, **draped** in black curtains, with some flowers in the school colours round its base. I must be **tripping**.

Mrs Randall catches my eye and nods at me. Miss Bardwell, I notice, doesn't catch my eye. No, her eyes are totally busy – **drilling** a big hole in the back of Nora's head.

The funeral **service** itself is *alright*, in the same way that some bad dreams are *alright* because they're not nightmares. At least I can't see or hear Miss Bardwell from where I'm sitting. I can hear every word that Onkel Dieter says, unfortunately. It's incredible. He talks through every minute of the church service. All I can hear is him saying

+++ to hiss – zischen +++ to hire – ausleihen +++ tribute – Ehrung +++ to drape – behängen +++ to be tripping – auf einem Trip sein +++ to drill – bohren +++ service – Gottesdienst +++

to Dad, "Was hat er gerade gesagt? Was heißt *pillar of the community*?" The Queen Mother must be suffering in heaven somewhere, if she's up there watching this.

But she'd be secretly pleased to see that everyone, I think, cries at some point during the hour and a half that the service lasts. Including Dad, who, even though he doesn't believe in God and didn't really believe in the Queen Mother, still can't stop the tears coming during *Jerusalem*. "Ein wunderbares Lied," he **coughs**.

I cry, too, of course. I cry when the vicar say things about the Queen Mother being *a good churchgoer, a fine human being*. And I cry when I think about what a *lousy human being* I am, in contrast. I couldn't feel any more guilty if I went into hospital and had a guilt transplant. My grandmother – was I ever nice about her? Was I ever grateful for all the money and effort she invested in me? **Nope.** All I ever did was **bitch about** her not kissing me and make fun of her being **deaf** and things.

I can't believe I've done nothing but feel guilty about being a bit interested in another boy for all these weeks but *not a bit* guilty about never being nice to my grandmother.

Oh, here I go again. More crying. Even the crying is still all about me. **Self-pity.** That's what guilt really is, right? It's all I've done recently, did you notice? Feel sorry for myself about nothing. Well, it stops right here, right now!

I look up at the **plaster** angels on the ceiling of the

✦✦✦ pillar – Pfeiler ✦✦✦ to cough – husten ✦✦✦ lousy – miserabel ✦✦✦ nope – nö ✦✦✦ to bitch about s. th./s. b. – über etw./jmdn. lästern ✦✦✦ deaf – taub ✦✦✦ self-pity – Selbstmitleid ✦✦✦ plaster – Gips ✦✦✦

church and I **make a vow**: *I will never again be so **selfish**. I will think about others and not just myself. I will be serious about my life and not **obsess about** boys.* Did you hear all that, God? Thanks.

The funeral service is finally over and we're all **spilling** outside into the churchyard. It's nice to be out in the fresh air. We're all supposed to go to a "**wake**" now – a sort of party after the funeral! – in a nearby restaurant. Before that, my mother orders all the Millington-Hausmanns to line up outside the church and shake everyone's hand. I'm not very enthusiastic: it will mean I have to speak to Miss Bardwell. But I don't have a choice.

I shake hands with about 800 people, it feels like, before Miss Bardwell appears in front of me. Luckily, she's not very interested in me: "So sorry, Emily. I have to get back to school … I won't be at the wake."

She's moving in for the kill, I know it, moving towards Nora, who's at the end of our family line up. I can hear that music from *Der Weiße Hai* in my head …

Nora looks surprised as Miss Bardwell reaches for her hand but she still shakes it. It's the first time they've met, of course, since the nightmare at Christmas, and the whole mess with Mr Michaels.

And then, rats! Mrs Randall's face appears in front of mine. "Emily, my dear!" she says loudly. "Such a tragic

---

+++ to make a vow – schwören +++ selfish – egoistisch +++ to obsess about s. th./s. b. – sich ständig mit etw./jmdm. befassen +++ to spill – *hier:* strömen +++ wake – Totenwache, *hier:* Leichenschmaus +++

loss. How are you bearing up?" I mutter, *Not too bad, thanks, Miss*, all the time trying to look past her. But Mrs Randall's hat is about the same size as Mount Rushmore and *is completely blocking my view of the Chalk Farm Reunion/Death Match* happening at the end of the line.

Mrs Randall talks and talks and then finally tells me one last time about the *great contribution* the Queen Mother made to Chalk Farm School and moves off. It's too late. I can just see Nora disappear out of sight, in the direction of her car. Miss Bardwell is getting inside a taxi that doesn't drive off but must be waiting for Mrs Randall.

Damn it, what did I miss???

✦✦✦ loss – Verlust ✦✦✦

A Million Miles from Home

The wake is over. All the sandwiches have been eaten. The world has been drunk dry of tea. There is not a cliché about death that I haven't heard. Onkel Dieter has done all of his card tricks and completely used up all of his Denglish. And Nora has completely vanished.

She's gone. She left the funeral after her **encounter** with Miss Bardwell and no one has any idea where she is. She didn't come to the wake and her mobile is switched off. "She probably just needed a little while to herself," says Mum slowly. "I don't think that mother's death has hit her yet." My own mother actually seems a bit better.

Then the rest of the family **pile** back **into** the black limousine still waiting outside and go home to The Grange. Max falls asleep on Dieter's shoulder. I close my eyes for a moment, too. I just want to get back and lie down for a bit on my bed. I have a terrible headache. And I'm hoping, of course, that Nora will reappear.

As we pull into my grandma's **driveway**, Dad mutters, "Da ist jemand."

+++ encounter – Zusammentreffen +++ to pile into – einsteigen in
+++ driveway – Auffahrt +++

Nora, I think, relieved ... though why isn't her car here?

"It's a boy," my mother says, frowning. "Maybe he's delivering more flowers ..."

The boy *is* carrying flowers, as it happens. Some yellow ones. He's standing **propped** in the doorway and **straightens up** as he hears the car.

It is Sam. A million miles from home. It's Sam.

He's just seen me, too, and he tilts his head to the side. He smiles nervously as my family pile out of the limousine,

+++ to prop – *hier:* sich anlehnen +++ to straighten up – sich aufrichten +++

one by one, all staring at him. He holds out his hand to me when I reach his side. "Sorry," he says. "I was late. I missed a bus and I had to **hitch a ride** with the fish van. My mum would kill me … Plus, I stink of fish, I'm sorry. Not a great first impression."

I hug him. It's true. He does smell like the sea. I think of that day on the beach we spent together in Scotland suddenly, how happy I was and how happy I am now to see him.

Sam's glasses are dirty, I notice, and, without thinking, I take them off his face and **polish** them on my yellow and **burgundy** tie. He smiles. "It's really weird to see you in your school uniform again."

He looks at me a bit shyly. My family are by now all standing in a circle nearby, staring openly at us. Sam's embarrassed. "Your phone was switched off. I didn't know where the funeral was taking place. I didn't want to bother you there anyway."

He seems a bit confused, somehow. "It was a bit of a spontaneous decision to come. I just really wanted to see you. I'm supposed to be at school on Monday and I've no idea how I'm getting home."

I don't say a word. Sam's come 667 miles (or is it kilometres? I always get them confused) to be here today. He didn't say a word about coming, he just did it.

"I just wanted to, well, **pay my respects**."

+++ to hitch a ride – mitfahren +++ to polish – polieren, *hier:* putzen +++ burgundy – burgunderrot +++ to pay one's respect – seinen Respekt erweisen +++

I don't say anything. I'm vaguely **aware of** Onkel Dieter watching me carefully. My parents are also looking Sam up and down in a funny way. They know he's the boy I was in Scotland with for ten days but that's about all they do know about him.

And, actually, even though I know I will have nightmares about this scene for years to come, I'm so happy to see Sam that I can't help it: I kiss him, **passionately**, in front of what is left of my whole family.

Somewhere near me I hear lots of noises: the wind in the trees, birds singing, my brother laughing, my father coughing, my mother gasping. And from somewhere up above, I think I even hear the Queen Mother's voice say, *Emily!* It's cool everyone – relax! We'll stop kissing in a minute. I'll face the music in a minute. But for that one sweet minute, just let me keep kissing the boy who cares about me so much that he'd travel all this way just to see if I'm OK. Please.

✦✦✦ to be aware of – sich bewusst sein über ✦✦✦ passionate – leidenschaftlich ✦✦✦

Von Joanna Thompson in der Reihe "Freche Mädchen –
Easy English!" ebenfalls erschienen:

Girls' School – *England Calling*
Girls' School – *The Ed Affair*
Girls' School – *Season of Love*
Girls' School – *Stand by your Sam*
Girls' School – *Vote for Love*

Thompson, Joanna:
Girls' School – Long Distance Kisses
ISBN 978 3 522 50135 4

Reihengestaltung und Gesamtausstattung: Birgit Schössow
Innentypografie: Kadja Gericke
Schrift: Minion und LTT Tapeside
Satz: KCS GmbH, Buchholz/Hamburg
Reproduktion: Medienfabrik, Stuttgart
Druck und Bindung: Friedrich Pustet, Regensburg
© 2010 by Planet Girl
(Thienemann Verlag GmbH), Stuttgart/Wien
Printed in Germany. Alle Rechte vorbehalten.
5 4 3 2 1° 10 11 12 13

www.planet-girl-verlag.de
www.frechemaedchen.de